Lather. Rinse. Murder

A Bianca Wallace Mystery, 3
(A Cozy Mystery Novel)

Lather. Rinse. Murder: A Bianca Wallace Mystery, Book Three
Copyright © 2023 by Daria White

PUBLISHED BY CRIMSON Fox Publishing
www.crimsonfoxpublishing.com[1]

FIRST EDITION
Cover Design by Vila Designs

eISBN: 979-8-215537-84-8

---

1.   http://www.crimsonfoxpublishing.com

ISBN (Paperback): 978-1-958051-23-8

Turner, Oregon

Lather. Rinse. Murder

A Bianca Wallace Mystery, 3

Lather. Rinse. Murder

A Bianca Wallace Mystery, 3

Chapter 1

"**Y**ou've changed your outfit three times already."

Bianca narrowed her brown eyes at her one and only sister, Melanie, who sat on the edge of her bed. Casper wagged his tail, staring up at Melanie, whose full eyelashes fanned her brown eyes, and her dark brown curls didn't go past her shoulders. "You're not helping. I'm nervous enough as it is."

"It's just a date. A date that you're finally going on," Melanie teased.

Bianca rolled her brown eyes. She had to cancel on Detective Sims—Lamar. The first time he'd asked her out the week prior. Moving into a new office space for Wallace Designs had been no joke, and thank goodness, he'd understood. They'd rescheduled for the following night, only this time, *he'd* canceled because he'd had to cover for another officer at the police station who'd had a family emergency.

Third time was a charm, right? Tonight was Friday night and only one date. At least that was what she repeated to herself to settle her quivering stomach. Grabbing the chilled glass from her nightstand, she took another sip of ginger ale.

"Thank you." Judging from Melanie's raised eyebrow, she'd picked up on her older sister's sarcasm.

"Anyway," Melanie continued, "I'm happy you're giving it a chance."

Bianca scratched at her jaw with her free hand. She'd said *yes* to a date with Lamar. When he'd called after she'd dropped her daughter, Alyssa, off at the airport to visit Alyssa's father, Malcom, and his wife in California for the summer, Bianca's ears had muffled at the detective's request. *Was he kidding me?* She'd thought. He hadn't been.

When she'd asked him to repeat the question, he had, and by his soft tone, he'd meant it. Nothing compared to his professional demeanor on his job. Self-assured. Stern.

When his gray eyes flashed in her mind, Bianca swallowed another gulp of ginger ale. How would she survive the night without acting like a silly teenager?

"You should go with the plum blouse you're already wearing," Melanie said. "It complements your brown skin tone."

Bianca nodded, tossing the black blouse on her bed next to her sister. She blew out her cheeks.

"You're going to be fine. You'll have a great time, and then tell me all about it." Melanie bounced on the bed.

Bianca eyeballed her. "This is not high school. We're not staying up late talking about our dates to each other."

"No, but I want to know if he kisses you," Melanie added.

Would he? A slow smile built on Bianca's lips. The most she'd figured was finding interesting topics to talk about. She didn't want to talk about the weather in Edenville. "You think he will?"

Melanie shrugged. "Every man's different, but if he forces himself on you, I wouldn't dare give him a second date."

Bianca wouldn't. No question.

"But if he's a gentleman, like I think he is… I think he'll ask to kiss you," her sister said, tilting her head to the side. "It's sweet when a man asks. That way, you have the choice to accept or reject it."

Bianca returned her glass to her nightstand. "Can I get through dinner first?" Leaning closer to her full-length mirror, she noticed one of her soft curls flattened. She'd spent an hour with the curling iron. "Ugh!"

She rushed back to the bathroom. Casper barked. She plugged the iron back into the outlet, and tapped her foot onto the tiled floor beneath her bare feet.

Her sister and Casper followed her and leaned against the doorway. "You look great, and I love the new hair color."

Bianca eyed her burgundy-berry highlights against her brown curls. Thank goodness Lillie's Hair Salon took walk-in appointments. "I wanted something different."

Melanie grabbed the iron. "He'll love it. Here. Let me help you."

Taking the flattened curl into her hands, Melanie went to work to perfect Bianca's hair.

Bianca rubbed at her arms. "I haven't been on a date in awhile." She sighed. "It's… been so long since I've liked a man this much."

"And he likes you back," Melanie pointed out. "I can tell."

Bianca exhaled. Detective—*Lamar* liked her. Even she couldn't deny it. Not with how he looked at her. Or the way they'd danced at the recent Blues & BBQ event in town. "It's going to be fine."

"Exactly." Melanie placed the iron back on the cream countertop. "Now shoes."

Bianca pointed to her dark-blue jeans. "Should I—"

"Those work perfectly, especially since the temperature dropped." Melanie tapped her finger on her lips. Then her eyes lit up as if she'd had a brilliant idea. "I got it! Your wedged ankle boots!" She dashed to her sister's closet and Bianca followed. Casper too.

Melanie bent to the carpeted floor and picked out Bianca's black ankle boots. "I know," her sister said. "I'm a genius."

Bianca giggled. "Fine. Thank you for being my stylist tonight."

When she heard a bell ring in the background, Bianca knew it was her timer on her phone, alerting her she needed to leave soon. "I have to go. I told him I'd meet him at the restaurant."

"Where are you two going?" Melanie picked up Casper and cuddled him close. He didn't mind the attention, but closed his eyes as she scratched behind his ears.

"Bello Italian," Bianca said, slipping her feet into her shoes after putting on ankle socks. "After that, he wouldn't tell me."

"Okay. So he wants to surprise you. I love it already!" Melanie had too much fun obsessing over her sister's dating life. Bianca would grill her sister later about her own love life, since she returned to the dating world, too. Not that she minded, since Melanie's recent suitor was Bianca's college friend, Jordan Thomas. At first, he had eyes for their mutual friend Nicole, but he accepted when she didn't feel the same for him.

"I'll text you when I'm on my way home." Bianca kissed her middle and index finger, and touched Casper's head.

"Have fun," Melanie said, following her to the door for the garage.

"I'll try." Bianca grabbed her keys and opened the door. Melanie didn't follow her inside the garage and for that, a release of bodily tension left her. She needed to gather her thoughts. She was going to a date. An actual date.

BIANCA PARKED HER CAR in the Bello Italian restaurant parking lot. For a Friday evening, it was no surprise that the parking lot was full, but Lamar had said he'd reserved their table ahead of time. Though she wouldn't have cared if they had to wait. They could have walked around Edenville's shopping center right behind the restaurant. Then again, perhaps it was a good thing they didn't have a long wait. Food could distract her.

Cutting the engine, Bianca exhaled. Her nerves were getting the best of her and her palms were sweaty. Rubbing them down her pants, she pondered calling and canceling. Had she been too presumptuous to think she was ready when she wasn't? Was this a mistake? She'd tried love before and it had ended in divorce, though she didn't regret having her daughter.

Alyssa. Her soon to be seventeen-year-old wasn't a baby anymore. She would go to college. Get married if she wanted and leave the nest. Where would that leave Bianca? Of course, Melanie lived with her, but that wouldn't be for forever. What if Melanie moved because she'd been reassigned as a journalist?

Bianca shut her eyes. Her thoughts were racing again. It was just dinner, but her fingers tingled. Her right knee bounced. It had been awhile since she'd dated, but she could do this. When her phone rang, she jumped. Pressing her hand to her chest, she wondered if it was Lamar. It wasn't. It was her mother, Deborah Wallace.

"Hey, Mom." Bianca put her on speakerphone as she checked her hair in her visor mirror.

"You're not bailing, are you?" her mother asked. "I'm calling to offer moral support. Melanie said you looked worried about your date. It's going to be fine, sweetie."

Though Bianca loved her close-knit family, this wasn't one of those times to intervene. "Thank you, but... I'll be fine."

"What did I tell you when you were younger? If he doesn't like you for you..." Her mother waited for Bianca to finish the statement.

"Then he's not the one," Bianca said. "Mom, I have to see if he's here. I have to go." She couldn't hang up fast enough, though she appreciated her mother's concern. "I love you."

"I love you too, and I want details." With that, her mother hung up.

When she heard a knock on her window, Bianca flinched but smiled when she saw Detective—*Lamar*. He flashed a bright smile, and suddenly, her nerves faded. Her brain turned to mush. If this was his effect on her now, imagine how she would react if he kissed her. She didn't say a word but unlocked the door.

He opened it for her. "Are you okay? When I saw you sitting here, I thought something was wrong?"

She shook her head, willing her voice not to squeak. "I'm fine." Good. She sounded like her usual self. Could he hear her heart palpitations? Was he feeling sweaty?

He closed the door after her, and she clicked on her car alarm. When she faced him, she took in his outfit for the evening. Short-sleeved gray collared shirt, complementing his gray eyes. Blue jeans, brown loafers, and his dark brown beard trimmed.

Bianca fought the instinct to brush her fingers against his chiseled face.

When he eyed her up and down, his lips parted. "You look great."

She brushed a curl behind her ear. "Thank you. You look... nice too." She had to get a grip!

Reaching toward her, he touched one of her curls. "You changed your hair color?" Then he dropped his hand back to his side.

Bianca felt the heat from his hand. "Yeah. I wanted something... different."

"It looks good on you." His eyes smoldered. Had his voice dropped?

"Thank you." She cleared her throat. "So, um... should we head inside?"

He held out his strong hand. "Ready when you are, *Ms. Wallace.*"

She smiled. "We're not being formal tonight, are we?"

"I'm kidding," he replied. When he motioned his head to her hand, Bianca realized she hadn't taken it yet.

"Sorry." She clasped his hand, enjoying how her palm fit in his. "I'll be honest with you... I'm a little nervous." She was past thirty. It was pointless trying to play that off.

He rubbed his thumb against her hand. "Can I tell you something?"

She nodded.

"Me too. Let's have fun and take the pressure off. You and me. Okay?"

Bianca breathed easier. He wanted her to be comfortable with him, and she appreciated that. "Agreed."

He motioned his head to the restaurant. "Let's go."

Not letting go of his hand, she walked in step with him. Tonight was free of expectations. She could be herself. He wanted that. Bianca did too.

Chapter 2

Bianca bumped knees with Lamar underneath their table. "Sorry about that."

He smiled at her. "It's okay." Then he winked at her.

Bianca's mouth went dry, but she swallowed despite the discomfort of her tongue sticking to the roof of her mouth.

"What do you want to eat?" His gaze focused on the menu.

Bianca took a sip from her glass of water before answering. "Perhaps the... fettuccine. I'm not sure yet."

He looked up from his menu and said, "Save room for dessert."

"I may skip that for next time." Had she just said that?

"Next time, huh?"

Bianca could not deny his flirtations with her.

"I—well—what I meant was..." She shut her eyes for a moment. "I'm not sure what I'm saying anymore."

He extended his firm hand across the table. "You're good. Okay?"

She sighed with relief. "Okay." Bianca continued to peruse her meal choices. "I will have the—"

"Is this how you treat all your customers?" a man yelled.

Startled, Bianca looked behind her shoulder. The man had to be in his late thirties, tall, olive skin, bald head with a full dirty blonde beard. He wore a black-and-white checkered shirt, covering a white shirt underneath with dark jeans.

"Sir," a server said, holding his hands out as if it would calm the customer down. He wore his short sandy hair in a low ponytail, wearing his black polo uniform shirt with black jeans.

There was a woman with the irate gentlemen at his table, but she stayed in her seat. She clutched her hands to her purse. Long, honey blonde highlights mixed with her black hair and dark-brown skin. She wore a plum blouse with black dress pants.

"I'm off duty," Lamar said, "but if he doesn't leave, I'm going to make him."

Bianca kept her eyes on the man.

"Fine!" the man yelled. "Fine!" He stormed out, and the woman at the table immediately relaxed.

Bianca wondered what had happened. What happened between the man and the server? Was the man dissatisfied with his food? What had caused his disruptive behavior? The woman present still didn't leave the table, so did something happen between them?

"I'll be back, Bianca." Lamar's chair scraped the floor as he stood. He joined the small huddle of servers and what looked like the manager.

Bianca set her menu down on the table, watching Lamar switch from her date to the officer. He checked on the woman after a few minutes with the staff. She gave a faint smile, but then pulled out cash from her purse. With that, she exited the restaurant.

Lamar stared after her for a moment, but he returned to his seat across from Bianca.

"What was that about?" she asked, her curiosity piqued.

"According to the server, the man who shouted, and the woman were arguing before we got here," he said.

Bianca pulled her lips in. She hoped the woman was okay. She'd looked terrified, judging by the way she'd clutched to her purse.

"Did you get any info from her?" Bianca wondered.

Lamar shook his head. "She wouldn't talk. That's part of my job, too. Some want help, while others don't." Then he leaned in, this time resting his elbows on the table. His eyes softened as he stared at Bianca. "I've had to learn when to let it go and… focus on *other things.*"

She momentarily forgot where they were. His gray eyes were too tempting, practically calling her heart to his. Swallowing to come back to her senses, she figured humor would bring her body temperature back to normal.

"Are you focusing on more important *things* now, Detective?" she asked.

He bobbed his head.

"Anything I can do to help?"

He shook his head. "Not unless you cover your face with the menu."

"That would defeat the purpose of this date… wouldn't it?" Then she raised the menu to cover her face. No harm in indulging the situation.

Lamar laughed aloud, and she placed the menu back on the table. "You're something, you know that?"

"I agree." She rested her chin on her palm.

His smile remained. "I'd like to discover more about you, too."

Her heart squeezed at the notion.

BIANCA CUT THE ENGINE to her car after following Lamar's silver Dodge truck to Edenville's creek one mile outside of town. After their dinner at Bello Italian, he'd recommended finding a quiet place for them to talk. Her choice of the Alfredo fettucine had been delicious, but she skipped dessert. Bianca hadn't expected the creek. She hadn't visited since high school. Lamar stepped out of his truck after parking beside her. Bianca smiled to herself, still not quite used to seeing him in normal clothes or outside of a police car.

Joining him outside, she took in the smell of grass, along with the water trickling over rocks and twigs. Drifting leaves and air bubbles floated lazily downstream, and when Lamar motioned to the nearby wooden bench, she sat next to him.

"What made you choose this place?" she asked. She was thankful for the cool breeze after a hot day.

He shrugged. "Sometimes I come here to think. I like the town park, but this space is not as crowded, I noticed. I'm assuming you've been here before."

Bianca nodded. "Not since high school, though."

"Did you ever go into the water?" He grinned.

Bianca stared at the water slipping over wet stones. The moonlight caused the stream to shimmer. "I don't think I did. I like nature, but not like that."

He chuckled.

"What? Would you go?" She gestured to the creek.

"Not my style, either," he said. "I'm more of a beach guy if I want to go swimming."

"When was the last time you went?"

He paused for a while. Did he not want to remember? "Long time ago. Before I moved here." Then the corners of his mouth perked up. "I never thought I'd like small town living, but this place is growing on me. It's... actually nice to be part of a community."

"I agree. I didn't appreciate it at first, either. We lived in Atlanta for a while, but when my dad... Well, my mother wanted a new start."

"I can understand that," he said. Then he moved closer, placing one arm around her shoulders. "Is this okay?"

"Uh-huh." Though she could barely breathe. "It's fine."

He asked, "So what are you going to do all summer with your daughter gone?"

That could take her mind off things. Alyssa had barely been gone a week, but Bianca did her best to give her daughter space and not call her every twenty minutes. Though Alyssa texted, they hadn't talked since she'd landed in California. Bianca wanted Alyssa to have fun. "Well, I'm still getting used to my office space. I like not working out of home. It was fine when I first started Wallace Designs, but as I continue to expand, I knew I would need a place eventually."

"Your family must be proud of you," he said.

"Yeah." If only her dad could see her now.

Lamar must have felt her tense up. "What's wrong?"

"Nothing. I'm fine." She faced him. "Thank you."

The moonlight flashed in his eyes. "For what?"

"For tonight." Should she tell him this was her first actual date in years? Her mother's match-ups didn't count since they didn't care to date a woman with a teenage daughter. No sense in hiding it. "This is the first date I've had in a long time. You've made it worth remembering, so thank you."

"I always want you to be comfortable with me, Bianca."

She giggled.

"What?" he asked, all serious.

"I keep thinking when we first met how you kept calling me 'Ms. Wallace,'" she reminded him.

"Why?" he asked. "Did that annoy you?"

She folded her arms over her chest. "Yes, it did, especially after I said you didn't have to."

He laughed. "I came around, though, right?"

"Yes." She nudged him. "Took you long enough."

He leaned in. "Are you trying to tell me you were eyeing me from the beginning? Is that why you wanted me to call you 'Bianca'?"

Her insides turned to mush. Clearing her throat, she brushed a curl behind her ear, needing something to take her mind off the way his deep voice flooded her body with warmth.

"I'll neither confirm nor deny that, but... it's not like I didn't notice you," she said.

"What *did* you notice?" he wondered.

"Hmm..." She tilted her head to the opposite side, making sure not to bump heads with him. "You're very focused at work, which the town surely appreciates. I think you're a brilliant detective."

His grin grew. "I'm listening."

"I also think you're a man of your word," she added.

"Thank you," he replied.

Bianca looked up at the night sky. The stars twinkled and a few clouds danced across the moon. The night had been perfect.

"You're persistent," Lamar said.

"What?" She turned to face him.

His smile reached his gray eyes. "You're persistent. I noticed that when your friend was accused of murder. You didn't stop until you found the answers. Do I think it's always a good idea...? No, but you have been an asset in the cases."

"Are you complimenting my police work, Detective?" she teased.

"Don't push it, Bianca." His eyes narrowed, but she could tell her teasing amused him. Then his gaze softened and his fingers rubbed small circles along her upper arm. Bianca's lips parted. Would he kiss her? Would he ask her or go for it? Though Bianca figured he wasn't the type of man to make her feel uneasy, was she ready to kiss him?

It was one thing to see each other in town. This was more... intimate. Her thoughts flitted between trust and worry. Placing her hand to her forehead, she cleared her throat.

"Are you okay?" His eyebrows furrowed.

"I'm okay." She didn't want to tell him she was playing the "what if" game in her mind. What if she wasn't ready? What would everyone in town say when they found out about them? Shutting her eyes, Bianca willed her mind to stop racing. It wasn't a marriage proposal. Melanie was right. It was one date. There was only one question she needed to answer now. Did she want to see him again? Her answer? *Yes.*

Turning back to him, she repeated, "I'm okay. Really."

"I was thinking the food made you sick." He smiled at her.

"No. A lot on my mind, but I'm fine. Thank you."

Then he checked the time on his wristwatch. "Oh, man. I lost track of time, and I work an early shift tomorrow."

"Yeah, I've got some new furniture pieces being delivered in the morning, so I have an early day, too," she added.

"I can't wait to see it when it's all finished," he said. "Glad it's working out for you."

"I appreciate that." Bianca stood to her feet.

Lamar followed, taking her hand in his once more. This time, he linked their fingers together. Bianca didn't mind at all, but her heart pounded as they made their way to her car. The rocks crumbled under their shoes, and when she unlocked her car, the beep interrupted the silence.

"Want to do this again?" he asked.

She exhaled. "I'd like that."

"I'll check my schedule and we can go from there. Okay?"

She looked up at him. "Works for me."

He used his free hand to cup her cheek. "You're beautiful, Bianca." He inched in closer and her eyes fluttered in anticipation, but to her surprise, he kissed her forehead. "Let me know *when* you're ready for me to kiss you."

Bianca gasped. He caught on to how tense she'd been. Though they'd shared a few laughs at dinner about their favorite movies and old TV shows, she couldn't deny her jumbled nerves. Despite it all, her chest expanded with pride. She'd taken the chance and said *yes* to a date. With time, she would get used to it.

The last thing she wanted was to face the greatest "what if?" What if Lamar was a good match for her and she didn't take the time to find out?

"Thank you," she replied. "I had a good time."

The corners of his mouth turned up. "Me too." Releasing her hand, he took a step backward. "I'll wait until you pull off before I leave."

Such a gentleman. Bianca turned to open her door, only to catch the moonlight reflecting off of something on the ground. She focused her eyes. Was it a watch? She squinted but it wasn't clear as it was in the daytime.

"Something wrong?" Lamar asked.

She shook her head. Perhaps someone had lost it and didn't know it. Maybe they'd come back for it. How long had it been there? "I'm fine. Thought I saw something." She faced him again. "Good night, Lamar."

"Good night, Bianca." With that, she slid into the driver's seat and started her engine. *Let me know when you're ready for me to kiss you.* Her heart melted.

Chapter 3

The garage to Bianca's modern farmhouse clanked as it opened. She'd made a quick stop at R&J's Restaurant and Bakery. Knowing Melanie, she'd ask her plenty of questions, so she'd picked up a new dessert Judy had made. Cookies inspired by Cookies and Cream ice cream. Bianca's mouth watered. She grabbed the pink box, cut the engine, exited her car, and made her way to the door. By the time she'd opened it, Melanie greeted her with a smile as big as the Cheshire cat from *Alice and Wonderland*.

"Here you go." She handed Melanie the box.

Her sister bounced on her toes as she took the treats. "Tell me everything!" She sat at the dining table.

Bianca took a seat alongside her, opening the box. "We had dinner."

"And? Details!" Melanie's eyes brightened with excitement.

"And then... sat and talked at the creek," Bianca replied.

"In the moonlight." Melanie touched a hand to her chest. "So romantic. I'm telling you, the simple things never go out of style. I love it!"

Bianca had to agree. Though she didn't mind a man surprising her on a date, it didn't compare to being present with her in conversation. Making her feel seen and understood. Lamar did that, and her heart was full drinking in the moment.

"So..." Melanie rested her elbows on the table.

"What?" Bianca bit into her soft cookie, knowing what her sister meant.

"Don't do that." Melanie's eyes squinted at her. "Did he kiss you?"

"No. Well, I take that back. He kissed me on the forehead."

"Really?" Her face fell.

"It was kind of sweet, Mel. Though I did my best to relax, I was a little out of my comfort zone tonight. I'm glad we're taking things slow. After my divorce, I'm not trying to rush anything."

"What did he say, though?" her sister pressed.

Bianca couldn't help but smile. "He said, 'Let me know when you're ready for me to kiss you.'"

Melanie's mouth dropped. "Wow."

"What?"

"I'm sorry, but that's attractive to me. That means he's willing to be patient with you. I'm telling you, a man will wait for what he wants."

Bianca swallowed her treat. "I believe so too. So... you called Mom?"

Melanie's eyes gazed upward. "I figured you could use a pep talk."

Bianca didn't care to be on display. Not even with her family. "I didn't plan to talk to mom right before Lamar showed up. I felt like a... teenager again."

Melanie's eyes met hers, and she nudged her shoulder. "We're only happy for you."

Bianca swallowed another mouthful of her cookie, holding back a moan. Good and bad at the same time. "Thanks. I'm glad I went."

"Will there be another one?" Her sister's eyes squinted at her.

Bianca wiped her mouth and hands with a napkin. "We'll see."

"THEY PICKED SOMEONE else?" Veronica, Bianca's virtual assistant, asked.

"Yes, they did." Bianca's meeting with a real estate company had gone well the week prior. Yet, they'd chosen another graphic designer.

Bianca blew out her cheeks, staring at her screen. Veronica video-chatted with her through Zoom every Monday to go over daily tasks and to check in on new projects Bianca needed to tackle next. If there was something pressing, they would correspond via email or phone. Working today on a Saturday was an exception.

Since they were planning a grand reopening, they had worked overtime to prepare. From updating the website, creating new business cards with the address, and sending out emails to current clients about her recent business changes. Bianca owed her assistant for working extra hours on a Saturday. Her hard work would reflect on her next check. Veronica's blonde hair was in a half up-do this time. Black mascara, accenting her dark-blue eyes, and blush lipstick covered her medium full lips.

"That's too bad," she said.

"That's part of the business." Bianca grabbed her water bottle. "Sometimes we nail it and sometimes we don't."

"Well." Veronica thumbed through what looked like her planner. "What about Luther Burkes? He runs Lather and Rinse Car Wash?"

"That's right!" Bianca snapped her fingers. Because of her work on her pitch to the real estate company, she had yet to follow up with Luther about creating graphics for his upcoming fundraiser. She nibbled at her bottom lip as she thought of a catchy title for the event. "Do you have ideas for a slogan?"

Veronica tilted her head to the side, her gaze looking upward. "What about... 'Clean wheels lead to...'" She giggled, facing Bianca. "Wait, a second. Remind me what the campaign is for?"

Luther had approached her after church the week prior, about a car wash to raise money for veterans. The idea had warmed her heart. He'd wanted her to make the fliers. Though her calendar filled quickly, Bianca wanted to make time for a worthy cause. "Helping veterans." She tapped a pen on her lips. Then her eyes bulged. "I've got it!"

Veronica jerked in her seat. "What?"

"Hear me out, okay? Let's tie it into the car wash name. 'Lather. Rinse. Make a Difference.'"

Veronica blinked.

Did she not like her idea? "What?"

"No, I like it. It's perfect! I'll make a note of it." She wrote inside her planner.

"Please do." Bianca laughed. Whenever she had great ideas, writing them down was a must. She lost count of the times her ideas had slipped away in the shower. Or waking up in the middle of the night and going back to sleep without taking notes. "So I'll follow up with him and say we're on board. If there's a good cause in Edenville, the people will line up to help. Once I get the designs printed, Luther can hang up the fliers."

"Great. Is there anything else we need to do today?" Veronica asked.

Bianca shook her head. "I think that was it. Do you have anything on your end?"

Veronica pulled in her lips, as if she were trying to hold back a smile.

"What? What's that face?" Bianca lifted an arched eyebrow in suspicion.

"I got a phone call this morning and..."

"And what?"

The bell chimed, alerting Bianca that a customer had walked into her office space.

"Sorry," Bianca said. "My next appointment is here. I'll have to talk to you later."

Veronica waved, signing off the video chat without another word.

Bianca stuffed her phone in her back pocket and sprinted to the door to greet her new customer. It wasn't whom she'd expected. It was Ms. Ella, who owned the floral shop in town.

"Hi, Bianca. I hope you're having a great Saturday afternoon." A smile covered her narrow, pink lips, which contrasted with her ivory skin. Her sundress complimented her full figure and her honey blonde hair grazed her shoulders.

"Thank you. Same to you." Her eyes locked on the bouquet of red roses in Ms. Ella's arms. "I'm sorry, Ms. Ella. There must be some mistake. I didn't—"

"These are for you, Bianca. Special delivery and I wanted to make sure you got them." The woman cheesed so hard, Bianca worried if her face hurt.

Blinking in disbelief, Bianca took the bouquet. "Thank you."

"There's a card. My assistant took care of the order, but I wanted to see how you looked when you got them. So romantic." The middle-aged woman blushed. "Have a good day, dear."

Bianca's mouth hung open, listening to her bell chime, when Ms. Ella had left her alone, standing on the carpeted floor. The fresh smell of roses tickled her nose, and Bianca grabbed for the card attached. Stuffed into a tiny white envelope, her stomach quivered with anticipation of reading it. It had to be Lamar. She placed the flowers on the coffee table in her sitting area for customers, and opened the note.

Thank you for last night.
I'm enjoying getting to know you.
I hope these roses send a smile to your face.
Lamar

She held back her girly squeal. Though she was sure Ms. Ella would spread news of her surprise gift all over town by church tomorrow, Bianca didn't care. Detective Sims—*Lamar* had done a sweet thing, and she appreciated it. She grabbed her phone from inside her pocket. No harm in telling him *thank you*. Perhaps she could bring a smile to his face at his job, unless he was solving a case. So far, nothing too heinous had occurred in Edenville since she'd helped bring the killer of supermodel Sherry Wilson, Melanie's childhood friend, to justice.

Bianca typed. *Thank you for the flowers.*

Sent.

In less than a minute, her phone vibrated.

Someone sent you flowers? You must have had a date.

He was teasing her? Bianca smirked. She'd play along. *If it wasn't you, then you must have some competition. His name is also Lamar, since he signed it. I might get you two mixed up.*

Don't play like that, Bianca!

She giggled. *Seriously. Thank you. They're beautiful.*

You're welcome. Have a good day.

You too!

She locked her phone screen. How could she concentrate on work now?

Chapter 4

While Lamar's gift left Bianca's curiosity awakened, she managed to focus on work. Because she'd worked through lunch, she walked to R&J's Restaurant and Bakery for a late lunch. It was only 2:00 p.m. on a Saturday afternoon, so not that late for her. She would usually enjoy the day off, but there would be plenty of time to rest after the reopening. She and Veronica could use a slight break. Speaking of a break, she knew Richard and Judy's peak hours at the restaurant, and today was a good day. Bianca didn't want to go to her friends' restaurant on a Sunday.

The bell chimed above her head as she walked through the glass doors. Judy, her redheaded friend, waved to her from behind the counter. She pulled her red hair into a low ponytail with a green headband. Perfect match for her emerald green eyes. With an apron wrapped around her small waist, she grabbed the pen from behind her ear. Bianca chose a table near the wall. Chatter from customers mixed with Brad Paisley's duet with Carrie Underwood, "Remind Me," filled her ears.

"I see you're back here. How were the cookies last night?" Judy asked, with a sparkle in her green eyes.

"Amazing, as always. I'll have to work it off later, but it was worth it." Bianca laughed. "You have a culinary gift."

Judy winked in reply to her friend's compliment. "What can I get you today?" She didn't bother giving Bianca a menu since Bianca had it all memorized, unless Richard came up with a new recipe as the chef.

"I'll take the Caesar salad, since I indulged last night." Bianca wrinkled her nose.

Judy laughed. "Coming right up." Then she leaned in with a whisper. "I want more details about the date."

Bianca coughed and tapped at her chest. "Right now?"

"I can take a break soon." Judy smirked and sauntered into the kitchen.

Bianca would have replied, but her phone rang. Was it Lamar? Didn't he need to concentrate on his job? Glancing at the screen, she saw her baby girl—almost seventeen-year-old baby girl. Alyssa. Bianca answered the video chat.

"Hi, sweetie!" She waved to her.

Alyssa—smooth, brown skin, soft brown curls, and a bright smile—greeted her mother. "Hi, Mom. Are you out somewhere? I hear... country music?"

Bianca giggled. "Having a late lunch at Richard and Judy's place. How are you? How's... California?" She still couldn't believe Alyssa was there with her father. They'd come a long way since her divorce from Malcom, but he'd remarried and they were trying to co-parent. A huge turnaround from how he used to be. He hadn't been as involved before. He'd blamed his work as an architect for his busy schedule, but he had changed and wanted to be a better father for Alyssa. Bianca ignored the faint sting inside her chest. The scar of divorce lingered even after she'd forgiven him and moved on.

"It's... huge. A lot different from Edenville. I don't think this place sleeps," Alyssa said. "I think I'm a small-town girl at heart, Mom."

Bianca smiled. "You'll get used to it, I'm sure. Have you seen any celebrities?"

Alyssa perked. "Not yet, but when I do, I'm so posting on Instagram. Chloe won't believe me otherwise."

Bianca released a satisfied breath. Good thing Alyssa wasn't forgetting about her friends since traveling to a new city. "I'm sure she'll love that. How are you and Kendrick?"

Kendrick was her daughter's boyfriend, and Alyssa worried their relationship would suffer with her gone. "So far, so good. We try to talk every night."

"That's great." Bianca played with her hoop earring. "How did the counseling session go?"

After Alyssa's kidnapping almost a month prior by Hunter Graham, Sherry Wilson's killer, Malcom had suggested Alyssa see a counselor for PTSD.

Her daughter shrugged. "It was okay. I didn't want to speak during the session at first, but Dr. Baylor is easy to talk to."

Bianca's heart warmed, grateful her daughter was recovering after a traumatic experience. Not to mention how Detective—*Lamar* had comforted her in the park where she, her sister, mother, and family friends had searched for Alyssa. He'd even come to Bianca's rescue when Hunter had kidnapped her. Bianca would never forget Hunter forcing her into his car at gunpoint.

Bianca smiled to herself, the red roses from Lamar coming back to her mind.

"Mom?" Alyssa said.

Bianca blinked. Daydreaming once again. She didn't want it to be a habit. It was too early to say anything and she could only hope Ms. Ella would keep her suspicions to herself. Then again, she'd said her assistant had taken Lamar's order, so unless she pried her employee for information, Ms. Ella had no news to spread around town.

"Do you need to tell me something?" Alyssa asked.

Bianca swallowed. Alyssa was old enough to know her mother was dating. "I... had a date last night."

Alyssa didn't blink. "With Detective Sims, right? I figured you would go out with him, eventually."

Bianca's mouth dropped. "How—what?"

Alyssa shook her head. "Come on, Mom. He's been to our house for dinner. The way you two stare at each other. Not to mention you two holding hands at the Blues & BBQ event."

Bianca's heart palpitated. Lamar had held on to her hand when the rain had ruined their town celebration of barbecue and blues music. "Yeah... that was something." She tucked a curl behind her ear.

"Uh, yeah, it was," Alyssa replied, but her gaze turned serious. "I'll be honest. I wanted you and Dad back together before... but I want you to be happy, Mom. And from the looks of it, Detective Sims seems like a good choice."

"We're not rushing anything," she reminded her. Alyssa bobbed her head. "So anyway, I hope you're having a good time out there. I miss you, though."

"Miss you too, Mom. I'll call you soon." She waved.

Bianca waved back. "Love you."

"Love you too." With that, Alyssa vanished from the screen.

"Here you go." Judy placed Bianca's Caesar salad in front of her. "That was Alyssa? You've got the Mom look."

Bianca sighed, grabbing her salad fork in her hand. "I guess I do, but at least she's having a good time."

Judy's green eyes softened. "You raised a good kid."

"Thank you." She took a bite from her salad. The crunch of the lettuce and the tangy dressing filled her mouth.

"Let the staff know if you need something. I have somewhere to be later today."

Bianca gave Judy a thumbs-up with her free hand.

Judy headed back to the kitchen. When Bianca's phone buzzed on the table, she checked the caller ID. Luther Burkes? She figured he'd beat her to following up about the graphic designs for the fundraiser. While she meant to call him prior, her previous client took up her time until her lunch break. She swallowed a mouthful of salad and answered.

"Hi, Bianca?" His raspy voice greeted her.

"Mr. Burkes," she said.

"You can call me 'Luther,' you know," he replied.

"I know, but if this is about your fundraiser graphics, I want to be professional if you're seeking my services," Bianca teased.

Luther Burkes laughed. "I should have known. I wanted to know—what? You mean you can do it?"

"Yes, I can," she confirmed.

"Well, all right then!" His voice perked up even more.

Bianca giggled, joining in his excitement. "Perfect! So the next thing to do would be to tell me your concept if you have one, unless you give me full creative control on the project."

Mr. Burkes paused. "Well... I'm not artistic like you, Bianca, but I was thinking of maybe tying in the American flag? Include some info about the cause for veterans, but not too wordy."

"Got it." Bianca nodded.

"Shoot, who keeps calling me?" he asked, sounding annoyed.

Bianca blinked. "I'm sorry? What?"

Mr. Burkes laughed, but he sounded nervous. "I'm sorry. The spam calls are too much. I know to block them, but some always slip through the cracks."

Bianca didn't pry. "I understand that. Spam calls are a pain. Well, I can have a mockup for you—"

"Can you hold Bianca?" Luther asked. "I have to take this one."

"Sure." *Ding.* Bianca turned at the bell to see Isaac Murphy walk inside the restaurant. He was Luther's manager at the car wash. Husky, stubbled-face, and his khaki shirt was untucked from his dark jeans. He walked to the to-go area.

"I'm sorry, Bianca." Luther chimed back in. "I have to go. I'll call you back when I get the chance. Okay?" Was he rushing her off the phone?

"Sure. No problem." He didn't bother to say goodbye and her phone beeped, alerting her the call had ended. Strange. One moment, he'd sounded excited. The next, nervous and in a hurry. Bianca only hoped things were okay.

She tucked her phone back inside her purse, just as Judy handed Isaac his to-go bag. He sauntered over to the smaller counter, holding the condiments. *Crunch.* Bianca took another bite from her salad.

Her eyes roamed from Isaac for a moment, but when he struggled to take his phone out of his pocket, she heard a *clink* on the floor. It looked like keys, and he didn't seem to notice. She swallowed and waved to get his attention. No use. He glued his eyes to his phone screen. Perhaps a text distracted him?

Bianca stood to her feet and hurried the few steps in front of her, bypassing fellow patrons eating at their tables. She bent down to pick up the keys, and to her relief, he met her hand with his.

"Thanks," he said. "I felt them missing from my pocket."

Bianca straightened to stand. "You're welcome. I just saw them fall."

Isaac straightened too, still being careful with his to-go plastic bag. He and Bianca made room for new customers entering. Thank goodness her table wasn't far away. She used her peripheral vision to monitor her purse.

"You know," she said. "I was just on the phone with your boss."

A dismissive laugh escaped his mouth. "He doesn't *trust me* to come back to work." He blinked when he realized his comment. "Sorry. It's been a... hectic day already."

Bianca shrugged. "No problem. We were discussing the fundraiser."

Isaac rolled his eyes. "Like giving back to the community will help his reputation."

Bianca's eyes widened. What did he mean by that?

Isaac checked the watch on his wrist. "Sorry I uh... have to go. He may have me call you to complete the designs for the fundraiser."

Bianca rubbed at her arms. "That's fine." She stepped backward. "I'm going to finish my lunch. Have a good one." His response about Luther had her mind questioning what he meant. It was probably nothing too serious. Perhaps the usual tension between employer and employee.

Isaac gave a slight wave and left. Bianca slid back into her seat. *Interesting... conversation.*

BIANCA'S OFFICE KEYS jingled in her hand as she reopened the doors to Wallace Designs. She kept the open sign flipped to *Closed*. Though she could head home now and pick Casper up from the dog sitter, she wanted to get a head start on Luther's graphics. Melanie would usually watch him, but with a new writing deadline, she needed to focus, without Casper interrupting her. She could already picture in her mind tying a car to the American flag theme, and when her creative wheels started turning, Bianca didn't want to forget. Locking the door behind her, she pivoted to face her office door.

The light was on. Hadn't she turned it off before going to lunch? Her eyes bugged. Was someone else here? Was she being robbed already? Scanning her sitting area for a weapon, Bianca grabbed the large, rose-colored painted vase filled with roses. Not much help, but what else could she use?

Her heart pounded when she heard murmurings. What did the thieves want? Her laptop? Bianca couldn't have that. Ducking behind her couch with the vase in one hand, she called Lamar. What made her forehead wrinkle was a phone ringing coming from her office? What?

She hung up. Lamar was here. Was he giving her another surprise on top of the flowers he'd sent her earlier?

Bianca stood to her feet. "Lamar?" she called out.

Her sister walked out instead, with a cake in her hands. "So much for a surprise." Behind her followed her mother, Judy and Richard, Jordan Thomas, and Lamar.

Bianca set her vase back on her coffee table. "What's all this?" Her eyes narrowed at Judy. "Didn't I see you already?" Then her lips quirked into a grin. "This is what you meant by *I have somewhere to be later?*"

Judy pointed to Melanie. "This was all her idea. I was to keep you in the restaurant."

Bianca squinted at Judy, but she couldn't deny the kind gesture from her friends and family.

Deborah Wallace approached her daughter, arms open wide for a hug. She maintained her pixie haircut and her brown skin glowed as usual. A few faint lines fanned from her brown eyes. "We wanted to do something special for you since you refused to have a party and invite the whole town."

Bianca didn't want the town to make a fuss over her reopening. They'd known about her business, but then again, having an official space was an accomplishment. She embraced her mother. "I don't need it, you know."

A smile crossed Richard Long's pale face. A flannel shirt hugged his husky built and his salt and pepper hair was thinning in the middle of his head. "We're proud of you, Bianca. No harm in letting us celebrating." He must have sneaked out with Judy, leaving the restaurant to the staff for a bit.

Jordan Thomas was next to hug her once her mother had stepped backward. An author and one of her best friends in college. "This place is amazing."

She embraced his muscular shoulders. Pulling back, she stared at his speckled eyes, crew haircut, and his full dark brown beard. "Thank you."

"Can I cut in?" Lamar asked.

Bianca's breath caught, but she exhaled anyway. "I didn't expect to see you here." She motioned to the door. "Don't you have crimes to solve?"

"I slipped away while on break, but I can't stay long." He pointed to her sister. "Melanie called and invited me, so I knew it had to be important."

Her sister rolled her eyes and set the cake on the coffee table. "Anyway, since the surprise flopped, we wanted you to know we're proud of you and we can't wait to see your business take off even more."

Bianca touched a hand to her chest. "I... I don't know what to say except... thank you. Thank you so much." Then she scanned the room once more. "Mom, you didn't invite Luther?" Luther was officially her mother's boyfriend.

Her mother pulled her phone from her purse. "I told him to be here." She held the phone to her ear to call him again. "It's going to voicemail. He must be busy at the car wash."

Bianca waved away her answer. "Don't worry. I'm going to stop by on my way home. I need to confirm some design ideas with him, anyway."

Richard grabbed Judy's hand. "We hate to run, but we have to get back to the restaurant." He waved goodbye to the group, along with Judy.

Bianca walked them to the door. "Thanks for coming." She pointed to Judy. "No more *secrets* next time."

"Can't promise that." She winked at her friend, then faced the rest of the group. "See you all later," she called out as the bell chimed when the door opened.

Jordan said, "I need to head out, too. Thanks again for the invite, Mel." When he leaned in and whispered in Melanie's ear, she giggled. Then he reached out to Bianca. "I can't wait to see it once you finish setting the place up." He kissed her cheek. Waving goodbye, he exited the door.

Bianca faced Lamar. "You too?" She waited by the door.

"You didn't get any cake," Bianca's mother said.

Melanie shrugged. "More for us."

"Thank you, Mrs. Wallace, but I have to get back to work," Lamar said.

"Well, thank you for coming anyway. I'm sure *Bianca* appreciates it." Her mother winked at her.

Bianca wanted to disappear into thin air, feeling like a teenager embarrassed by her mother in front of her crush. She forced a smile, facing Lamar. "I'll see you outside." He followed behind her, the bell chiming once more. They were alone but she kept in mind the glass windows. "I appreciate you coming. The flowers were more than enough."

"You're welcome," he said. "Although I wish I could stay—"

"I understand." He'd gone out of his way, and that had spoken wonders to Bianca.

"I'll call you later?" He raised an eyebrow, as if hopeful of her answer.

"I look forward to it," she replied.

He took her hand, running this thumb across her knuckles. "Have a good day, Bianca."

"You too," she said, breathless.

Chapter 5

Bianca swallowed the scrumptious red velvet cake, allowing the sweet treat to dance across her tongue. Buttercream icing was her favorite and Judy was a pro at making it. Her mother sat across from her in a cushioned chair, while Melanie sat beside her. Bianca's heart warmed again at the thought of her sister inviting her friends to celebrate her new business venture.

If only Nicole and Chad had been here, but they hadn't returned to Edenville from their honeymoon in Rome, Italy. Then they extended their trip to London, England. Bianca didn't blame the newlyweds for taking their time to return home. Being focused on a new spouse wasn't bad, especially after the scandal with Chad's stepfather's murder. His own mother, Priscilla, had orchestrated the killing, so no one could blame the couple for basking in their newfound happiness.

Bianca's mother checked her phone after setting her empty paper plate on the coffee table. "I don't understand why I can't reach Luther. He should have called me back now."

Melanie waved away their mother's comment with her plastic fork. "Don't worry, Mom. I'm sure he's busy. Remember, he's got that big fundraiser coming up for the veterans. You know what it takes to organize something big in this town."

Bianca agreed.

Deborah Wallace frowned. "I know, but..."

"What?" Bianca asked.

Melanie raised an eyebrow. "You two aren't... having any problems. Are you?"

Bianca hoped not. Her mother touched her hand to the new silver heart pendant necklace Luther had gifted her with. This was the happiest Bianca had seen her mother since their father's death. Hopefully, Luther wasn't playing her mother for a fool.

Her mother shook her head. "Oh, nothing like that. I trust Luther. He's a good man. It's just..."

"What?"

"He told me that his daughter had reached out to him this past weekend. She's in town."

Melanie blinked. "They're on speaking terms now?"

Bianca bobbed her head. "That's what he said the last time we asked him about his family."

Deborah Wallace rubbed her hands together. "Well... he didn't tell me everything. It's still a sore spot for him. He's not... *proud* of his past, but what if his daughter wants to make amends now?"

Melanie ran a hand through her shoulder-length, dark-brown curls. Her off the shoulder blouse showed her toned shoulder, and her dark fitted jeans complemented her slim frame. "He may need time to work things out with her."

"I wonder what changed his daughter's mind," Bianca added.

"From what Luther told me," her mother continued, "she wasn't on good terms with her husband—now ex-husband. Luther told me he'd warned her about him. Something about his demeanor didn't sit right with Luther. I guess she didn't care about his opinion. What if she wants to reconnect since it turned out he was probably right? Luther didn't tell me much more than that."

Bianca remembered the woman at the restaurant. She'd looked terrified of the man the staff had forced to leave. No one should have to live with that fear. Hopefully, Luther's daughter wasn't going through the same thing.

Deborah Wallace gave a faint smile. "I'm sure it's nothing, and he's busy with work as usual. I'll call him later."

"Or... I can go check on him," Bianca offered. "I need to finish some things with him anyway before the car wash. I have an idea for the design, but I always make sure I satisfy my clients."

Her mother's smile grew larger. "Thank you, sweetie. Just... don't tell him I wanted you to check up on him. He doesn't like me to worry."

"You're welcome." To lighten the mood some, Bianca changed the subject. "Thank you again for doing this." She gestured around the office. "I have to get used to working from an actual office space."

"I still say you need a grand reopening party. Judy and Richard can cater. I can find you a great photographer and—"

Bianca shook her head. "Mom, I'm trying not to be overwhelmed as it is."

Melanie interjected. "Honestly, sis. I think it's a good idea. It's an excellent opportunity to network. You can have Veronica advertise it for you online, so not only are you attracting new customers, you're giving our community a chance to see what you do."

Bianca desired a reopening, since she'd never had an official one. Wallace Designs had started in her kitchen, just Bianca on her laptop, experimenting with her drawings. Who knew starting a business from home would lead to a brick-and-mortar location? She still couldn't get over designing the graphics, pamphlets, and fliers for the trending Clique Classic clothing line. That had solidified her decision to expand.

"I'm great at planning events, dear. You won't have to worry about a thing. All I would need is a copy of your business logo to put on the invitations," her mother offered. "A small event is fine, but why not make it bigger? Get the whole town involved along with your clients?"

Bianca's heart pounded with excitement. She'd planned with Veronica to keep the reopening simple, but why not take the plunge and celebrate? "Well... if I'm going through with this, might as well do it right? Okay. Let's do it. Wallace Designs' grand reopening."

Melanie squealed. "I can even write a featured article for it!"

"Really?" Bianca wondered, her smile growing larger.

"Why not? I can make time between stories," Melanie said. "In fact... I've been thinking about starting my own online magazine. I don't know what my focus will be. Perhaps more inspirational pieces... I'm not sure yet. It's still fresh in my mind."

Bianca blinked. Had she heard her sister correctly?

"Melanie that sounds amazing!" their mother replied.

Melanie clasped her hands together. "I have a strong following online. Why not go for it?" Then she faced her sister. "Seeing you work your own business, the freedom you have as an entrepreneur, you've inspired me. I... I want to write on my own terms. Maybe... even a book?"

A book? Bianca's chest expanded with warmth. Her sister hadn't mentioned writing a book before. Had someone else inspired this talk of a change in her career? Could Jordan Thomas, a fellow author, be a motivator as well? Bianca didn't pry for now, but she would, especially since Jordan visited her home to spend time with her sister almost every weekend.

Bianca swallowed, taking all the new information in. "I'm happy for you, Mel." She supposed she wasn't the only one with recent changes happening in her life.

BIANCA LOCKED HER OFFICE doors for the evening. First stop: Luther's car wash. Thank goodness Melanie had agreed to pick up Casper from the dog sitter. Bianca's royal-blue Kia Soul beeped as she unlocked her doors, and sliding into the driver's seat, she couldn't wait to get home and soak in a hot bath.

After messaging Veronica about the grand reopening party her mother and sister had talked her into, Bianca had spent a few hours completing some sketches for Luther. Veronica hadn't responded yet to her message, so she used the valuable time to work. Thankfully, she'd talked to Luther herself earlier. If he wanted too many changes, she'd have to start from scratch, but she was sure one of her designs would convince him.

Cranking the engine, she backed out of her parking space and turned onto Main Street. Bianca passed the post office, Parks Deli, and Ms. Ella's Floral Shop. The traffic light stopped her, and her car rang since she'd connected her Bluetooth. Lamar's name and number showed on her screen. She smiled, and while she hadn't expected him to call this soon, she didn't hesitate to answer.

"Are you done with work today?" She turned into Luther's Lather and Rinse Car Wash, spotting the drive-up bays. Pink hues of purple and orange illuminated the sky as the sun set. Bianca didn't spot any cars, so Luther must have closed for the day.

"Got some paperwork, but after that, I'm heading home," his deep voice replied. "How about you? Good day?"

Bianca cut the engine. "I think so. I'm at Luther Burkes's car wash. Want to get his opinion on my design ideas."

"Want me to call you back?" Lamar asked.

She locked the door behind her, after grabbing her sketches and adjusting her Bluetooth in her ear. "No, you can keep me company until I see him. He might be in his office."

"Sure you're not being a little selfish, Bianca? Wanting to keep me on the phone?" he teased.

A *tsk* escaped her mouth. "You're such a flirt, *Detective Sims.*" She couldn't contain her smile.

"I think you like it, *Ms. Wallace,*" he said.

Bianca inhaled the moist air, while listening to the gurgle of the draining system. "I won't give you the satisfaction of telling you *if* I do."

He chuckled.

Bianca laughed, only to gasp. Her eyes bulged. Adrenaline shot through her system.

"Bianca?" Lamar said. Judging by the shift in his tone, he figured something was wrong. "Bianca?"

"La-Lamar." Bianca stared at a body. Facedown inside the car wash over the floor grate. Bullet holes were in the wall.

"Tell me what's going on." His voice was stern this time. He'd switched from playful Lamar to Detective Sims.

Bianca exhaled, willing her body to calm down. "There's a man inside the car wash. Facedown. He's not moving." Inching closer, she saw how the water soaked his dark jacket, but there was blood and a hole that punctured it. A bullet wound. Who shot him? Had she heard anything as she'd pulled up? Where was Luther? "I think someone shot him, Lamar."

"Bi-Bianca?" Luther's raspy voice caught her attention.

Her head jerked to see Luther in the corner of the wash bay. How had she not seen him? "Luther?"

"What... What happened?" he asked, sweat beading on his wrinkled brow.

"Bianca?" Lamar said.

Bianca opened her mouth to speak until she saw a gun in Luther's hand. Her mouth went dry. "Lamar..."

"We're on our way," he said. "Stay on the line, Bianca, okay?"

Her voice was barely audible because of the scene. "Okay."

Chapter 6

Bianca sat on the hood of her car. Lamar, Detective Atkins, and several other officers had arrived at the scene. The ambulance arrived at the car wash before the police did, since the station was further away. Someone apparently knocked out Luther since the paramedics discovered a small bump on the back of his head. Bianca tapped her heel to the ground. She couldn't figure why Luther had had a gun in his hand.

Deciding to return to the place where she was standing earlier, she watched the EMTs turn the body over, face up. Bianca blinked. Her eyes shifted to find Lamar.

"Detective Sims?" she called out.

He faced her and held up his index finger. He and Detective Atkins were questioning Luther. Bianca's gut wrenched. She wasn't convinced he'd killed the man lying in front of her, and if he had, why hadn't he killed her when she'd spotted the gun in his hand? Bianca wrung her fingers together. This was supposed to have been a meeting with her latest client, while also checking in on her mother's significant other—not her discovering another dead body.

"This is becoming a habit with me," she said to herself.

"What?" Detective Sims replied.

She pointed to the man on the ground. "Isn't that the man from the restaurant?"

Lamar edged closer. "Oh, wow, you're right." He made a note on his pad.

"Did Luther recognize him?" Bianca wondered.

"Not sure. He's a little disoriented from the blow to his head." A *tsk* escaped his lips. "And we got an anonymous tip to come back here, too."

Bianca replayed what he'd just said. "You got an anonymous tip? Someone called? You mean to tell me the police didn't—"

"Yes, Bianca, we got a call. We were going to send out a squad car, but we got called for another emergency." He tapped his pen on his notepad. "Can we get back to it, please? Did you see anyone else here when you pulled up?"

She couldn't ignore her suspicions. Who had called? Did the anonymous caller commit the crime and then lead the police to Luther? Bianca answered Lamar anyway. "No, not that I can remember." She squared her shoulders, knowing what was coming next. "Am I a suspect?"

He didn't answer her direct question, but motioned for her to follow him away from the body. "Why were you here again, Ms. Wallace?"

She rubbed at her bare arms, remorseful as she'd worn a sleeveless shirt that day. "I came to show some graphic designs to Luther. He wanted fliers to go out advertising his car wash fundraiser next week. He's raising money for veterans."

"What time did you get here?"

He'd been on the phone with her, but this wasn't the time to tease him. "It was close to 6 p.m. Perhaps five till six?"

"I can confirm that," he said. "Next?"

"I walked over to the wash bay, looking for Luther. I was about to go to his office when I saw the body."

"Did you touch it?"

"I only looked closer to notice a bullet wound."

"Did you hear a shot of any kind?" he asked.

Bianca's eyebrows furrowed. "No. I don't remember hearing gunshots despite the bullet holes in the wall. Has he been dead long?"

"The medics haven't said." Lamar sighed. "If he's the same guy from the restaurant, it makes me wonder how Luther knew a *jerk* like that."

Bianca snapped her fingers. "What about the woman he was with?"

Lamar shrugged. "What about her? You saw her?"

"No, but—"

"No theories, Bianca, please." He squeezed his eyes shut for a moment.

She raised her hands. "Listen for a second. It was obviously an argument that stirred things up to get him that angry. What if this woman followed him? Maybe this was her way of making sure he didn't bother her again."

"That's speculation, Bianca." Lamar stuffed his notepad into his back pocket. "Besides, why involve Luther?"

"That part, I haven't figured out yet," she said.

He rested his hands on his hips. "It's best you go home. If you can remember anything factual that I can use, call me."

Bianca stared into his gray eyes. He was right. She didn't have enough information to continue, so it was best to go home and rest. Tonight had differed from what she'd expected it to be. "Okay." She turned to walk to her car, but he reached for her.

His gray eyes softened. "I'm glad you're okay."

She gave a small smile. "Thanks for coming so quickly."

He didn't say a word, but tires screeching in the background broke the moment between them. Bianca's mother practically jumped out of her 2018 Silver Metallic Chevy Equinox. "Bianca!"

She ran to her mother and embraced her tightly. Though she'd stayed on the line with Lamar until the police arrived, she called her mother next. Her mother's voice sounded shaky after Bianca shared someone had hurt Luther. She didn't want to tell her too much over the phone, but her mother hurried to the scene, leaving her dogs with a neighbor.

"Are you all right? Where's Luther?"

Bianca pulled back and pointed to the ambulance truck, where Luther sat, holding an icepack to his head.

"I have to see him." She pivoted, but Bianca held her back.

"Mom, wait." How would she tell her the rest?

"What?" Her mother's jaw clenched.

"Mrs. Wallace," Lamar said as he came from behind Bianca. "There's... been a murder."

Deborah Wallace's eyes widened. "What? Who?"

"Do you know if Luther knew a Ronald Cartwright?"

Her mother shook her head as Bianca squeezed her mother's hand. Her mother said, "The name doesn't ring a bell. Was Luther attacked, too?

"Yes. That or he fell, but we..." Lamar exhaled. "Someone killed our victim with a gun. We found Luther holding that gun. Because of the blow to his head, he can't recall what happened yet."

"You don't think he did this? He couldn't have. Luther's not a killer," her mother said, practically pleading for his innocence.

Lamar didn't reply to her comment. "We'll have to bring him in for further questioning."

Bianca's mother touched a free hand to her forehead. "Can I at least talk to him before you do? Please?"

Detective Sims nodded, and Bianca released her mother's hand. She sprinted to Luther's side, embracing him.

Bianca touched a palm to her chest. She faced Lamar once more. "You're not going to... arrest him, are you?"

"I can't tell you that. You found him next to a dead body. No one else was here, but we'll do a formal prints match. Unless we find something different, Luther is a suspect."

Bianca nodded. "I understand." *Was the gun even Luther's?*

"Why don't you head home?" Lamar suggested.

"I can't leave my mom here," she said. "I can't imagine what she's feeling right now."

"Sims!" Detective Atkins called out, waving him over.

He held up his finger. "One sec." Then he faced Bianca. "I have to go."

Bianca bobbed her head, and when he walked away, she released a deep breath. Only one question played in her mind: Was her mother's boyfriend... a killer?

ONCE SHE'D ENTERED her house, Bianca stepped out of her chunky heeled pumps. The cool hardwood floors soothed her, and she sighed with relief. Casper barked at her return, and she knelt to pet her Beagle. Scratching behind his ears, she relished in his company.

"Is it true?" Melanie asked as she stood from the couch in the living room.

Bianca heard the TV in the background, and she rose to her feet. Casper trotted to his water bowl. "It's on the news?"

Melanie bobbed her head. "No details yet, but they said they found a body at Luther's car wash." Her sister frowned. "How's Mom?"

"She went to the hospital with Luther. They want to keep him overnight for observation since he got a bump on his head."

Her sister returned to her seat on the couch, and Bianca sat beside her.

"Wait a minute." Melanie tilted her head to the side, facing Bianca. "Did you... You were there, weren't you?"

Bianca shrugged.

Melanie groaned, covering her face. "What is it with you and stumbling on crime scenes?"

Bianca raised her hands. "I wish I hadn't been at this one."

Her sister dropped her hands from her face. "What happened?"

"I wanted to meet with Luther about the designs. Next, there's a body on the ground. Dead."

Melanie's eyes widened. "And Luther?"

"He was holding the gun, but it looks like he doesn't remember," Bianca said.

"Who else could have been there?" her sister wondered.

"Lamar's working on that. He said there was an anonymous call earlier, before I got there."

"Will you get involved this time?" Melanie asked.

"Not with the grand reopening coming up soon. Besides, it was too close a call last time with Alyssa. I... don't want to do that again, no matter how much I want to help." Bianca would never forget the way her daughter had screamed when Hunter Graham had held her captive. The pain of almost losing her daughter last time had been too much.

Melanie rubbed at her forehead.

Did her sister have something on her mind? "What?"

Her sister asked. "What if... we had Luther all wrong, Bianca?"

"What do you mean?" Bianca's pulse thrummed at the idea. Sure, they were still getting to know Luther, but he didn't appear dangerous.

"I *mean*," her sister said, "he appears to be a nice guy, but what if he *did* this? Think about it. Mom says he doesn't talk much about his past. What if... this is him showing his true colors? Perhaps Mom needs to get away from him."

Bianca's thoughts scrambled to understand, too. "Mom's not naïve. She wouldn't be dating Luther if she thought something was off about him."

"What if he's a talented actor, Bianca? Can you imagine the many women fooled by men they care about?"

Bianca's chest tingled. "I don't... I can't bring myself to believe that... Not after..."

"After what?" Melanie touched a hand to her arm. "What?"

"On my date with Lamar, a man was asked to leave the restaurant. I guess things got heated between him and the woman he was with. She looked terrified," Bianca explained.

"How does that relate to this?"

"That man was killed tonight. His name is Ronald Cartwright."

Melanie's eyebrows furrowed. "Ronald Cartwright. Why does the name sound familiar?" She grabbed her phone from the coffee table and did a Google search. "Wow."

"What?" Bianca leaned in to read along.

Melanie read aloud. "Ronald Cartwright. Top Real Estate Mogul in Texas. His sales from last year totaled over $1 million. We did a feature on him last year since he donated $250,000 to a children's hospital."

"So what's a big-time real estate guy doing in a small town like Edenville? Anything about his personal life?" Bianca asked.

"Married once but separated and later divorced, filed by his wife."

Bianca used her index finger to scroll down the screen. There had to be photos, right? She stopped once she saw Ronald Cartwright next to a beautiful brown-skinned woman. "Oh, my goodness."

"What?" Melanie faced her.

"This was the woman at the restaurant." Bianca read further. "Camille Burkes Cartwright."

Melanie gasped. "You think...?"

"Lamar and I saw Luther's daughter," Bianca said.

Chapter 7

The following Sunday morning, Bianca and Melanie attended Edenville Community Church without their mother. Despite a few murmurs and whispers, most of their friends showed concern for their mother. The sisters thanked them for their kind words. Entering the parking lot, Melanie adjusted her purse strap.

"Do you want to check on Mom at the hospital?" she asked.

Bianca agreed. "Maybe we can convince her to come eat with us? It's not like her to miss cooking a family meal."

"True, but things are… different at the moment," Melanie said. "I still can't believe this is happening."

They walked side by side to Bianca's car.

"Bianca!" a familiar voice cried out.

Both women stopped to spot Judy carrying what looked like a dishpan covered with foil.

"What's this?" Bianca wondered.

"Taco casserole. It's still warm." She handed it to Melanie. "I heard what happened on the news and with your mother not being here, I thought I'd make her something. Are you heading to the hospital?"

Bianca nodded. "We thought we'd check in on her and Luther."

Judy raked a free hand through her red hair. "I hope the police clear this up, and soon. There're already rumors going around about Luther."

"Like what?" Melanie asked.

Judy's lips thinned, but she continued. "Well... no one knows much about his past, only that he came to town to start his business ten years ago. He talked about having a daughter and granddaughter, but nothing beyond that."

Bianca's teeth pulled on her bottom lip. "Has anyone met his daughter?"

Judy shook her head. "I never have."

Not much information to go on there. Bianca smiled at her friend. "Thank you for the casserole. We'll tell our mom you made it."

Judy's green eyes sparkled. "You're welcome. I'll talk to you later."

Bianca bobbed her head and Judy walked away. Then she faced her sister. "Let's go."

They got in her car. The drive to the hospital had little to no traffic.

"I still wonder..." Melanie said, adjusting in the passenger seat. She balanced the foil pan on her lap.

"What?" Bianca tapped her fingers on the steering wheel.

"Is Luther... hiding something?"

Bianca sighed. "Just because he's not as talkative as Ms. Ella doesn't mean he's hiding something."

Melanie rested her elbow against the passenger window. "Something doesn't feel right, Bianca. What if there's more to it? Mom's possibly dating a—"

"We need *evidence* first." Bianca commented.

Her sister eyeballed her. "You said you weren't getting *involved* in this case."

"I'm not. I'm only saying we can't assume anything. Luther's a great guy from what I've seen, and I don't think he's capable of killing someone." She tapped the brakes to stop at a red light, only to have it turn green, so she coasted through the intersection.

"Bianca!" Melanie screamed.

BEEEEEEEP! Slamming the brakes, Bianca stopped before hitting another car. A beige Buick. They didn't stop running through a red light.

Melanie touched a hand to her chest. "Some people."

Bianca's breathing eased. The car almost hit them. "Are you all right?"

"Yeah. Let's get to the hospital."

Bianca proceeded down the street, wanting to get to her mother's side. Cars crowded the hospital parking lot, but she found a spot in the visitor's section. There was a police car a few spaces away, and Bianca could only imagine Lamar having an officer watching Luther as he recovered. Cutting the engine and locking the car, she and her sister entered the hospital through the automatic doors. Melanie carried the casserole dish and Bianca figured her mother would appreciate the kind gesture from Judy.

They bypassed the small alcove waiting area with plastic chairs around a table covered with magazines and newspapers. At the front desk, they spotted a woman in scrubs hanging up the telephone. She'd tied her black hair into a bun, and the faint freckles that covered her nose wrinkled as she gave them a bright smile.

"Can I help you?" she asked.

"We're here to see Luther Burkes," Melanie said. "Our mother is here. Deborah Wallace."

The nurse's face softened. "He's in Room 103, but there's a police officer outside his door. I can't help you if he refuses to let you in."

Bianca nodded. "Thank you."

Melanie led the way down the hall. The fluorescent lights buzzed and the smell of coffee mixed with hand sanitizer filled Bianca's nose.

"I guess that's it." Melanie gestured to the room ahead that had an officer sitting outside the door. Was that necessary? Did they assume Luther was a dangerous criminal? Bianca didn't recognize the officer, but perhaps she could persuade him, since she knew Lamar. Could Luther have over one visitor inside his room?

"Excuse me?" Bianca said.

The officer stood to his feet. He looked only 5'9", husky, and had a dark brown mustache against his brown skin. "Can I help you ladies?"

"Is Deborah Wallace inside?" Melanie asked. "She's our mother. We're also friends of Luther Burkes."

He pointed to the dish in Melanie's hand. "What's that?"

Melanie undid one side of the foil-covered pan. "Taco casserole."

He exhaled deeply. "Wait here." He took a few steps away from them and talked into his walkie-talkie.

Bianca tuned in to listen while Melanie leaned against the beige wall.

"I've got two women wanting to see the suspect," he said.

Suspect? Well, until more clues surfaced, Luther was the police's only option.

"Last name Wallace," he continued.

"What does he think we're going to do?" Melanie whispered. "Hide a knife inside the casserole so Luther can escape?"

Bianca held back her giggle. "It happens."

"Bianca? Melanie?" Deborah Wallace stepped outside of Luther's room. Her eyes were red, either from crying or staying up late the night before. Bianca's heart broke for her mother. Deborah Wallace hugged both of her daughters, but it was awkward for Melanie since she carried Judy's dish. "You didn't tell me you were coming." She pointed to the dish once she stepped back. "What's this?"

"A taco casserole. Judy made it for you and since we're not having our usual family dinner..." Melanie shrugged and their mother hugged her once more.

"I'm sorry." She sniffled and took out a handkerchief from her jacket pocket. "It slipped my mind. I slept on the couch inside Luther's room."

The officer turned and faced the women. "I'm sorry. Only one visitor inside the room." He focused on their mother. "Are you leaving, Mrs. Wallace?"

Her mother's eyebrows dropped with apparent fatigue. "No, Officer Butler. I'm going with my girls to the cafeteria." She motioned for them to follow her.

Bianca and Melanie walked in step with their mother.

"Mom, you need to get some sleep," Bianca said.

They entered the cafeteria with dozens of circular tables and plastic chairs. Chairs scraped the floors as hospital staff, patients, and visitors sat and rose from their seats.

Melanie set the pan dish on an empty table. "I'll get us some plates and silverware." She touched the side of the pan. "It's still warm."

Bianca smiled after her and sat next to her mother.

Deborah Wallace rubbed her handkerchief along her nose again and used the small hand sanitizer on top of the table to clean her hands. "This is the longest night I've had in a while."

Bianca reached out and touched her mother's wrist. "Has anyone come by to visit Luther since you've been here?"

Her mother sniffled again. "Detective Sims and Detective Atkins. When they left, they assigned Officer Butler to keep watch."

"When Luther's discharged, what will they do?" Bianca asked.

Her mother sighed. "Take him... into custody. He had the gun in his hand, Bianca. It's registered to him. You're a witness to that. Unless something changes, Luther could go to jail for... murder."

Bianca's chair scraped the floor as she scooted closer to her mother. She draped an arm around her shoulders. "It'll be okay, Mom. Detective Sims will find out who did this."

Her mother patted her hand as Melanie sat down with the white paper plates and plastic silverware.

Her eyes grew wider. "Mom?" She scooted her chair close too.

"I'm sorry." Deborah Wallace wiped at her eyes. "This is just... bringing up memories. I remember praying for strength when your father..." She choked back her tears.

Bianca held back tears inside her own eyes. She didn't consider this case triggering her mother. The emotional toll Bianca's father going to jail because of a case of mistaken identity had taken on her mother. Before proving his innocence, he'd died. He hadn't lived to see justice prevail on his behalf. Why was this happening again?

"Mom, I'm so sorry," Melanie said.

"No, it's not the same, but..." her mother said. "It's hard to watch this."

Bianca raised her head from her mother's shoulder. "Did you hear Luther give his testimony to the police?"

Her mother answered. "He told the police that he was working late that night. He and Ronald argued."

Oh, no. That didn't make Luther's case any better. Bianca's stomach churned.

"Did they physically fight?" Melanie wondered.

Deborah Wallace bobbed her head.

"What about the gun?" Bianca asked.

"That, he's not sure. During the struggle, a few shots were fired, but no one was hit. That must have been when Ronald knocked him out. When he woke up, he saw you and the gun in his hand," her mother explained.

"But I don't get it." Melanie rested her chin on her palm.

Deborah Wallace's face pinched.

"Mom?" Bianca tilted her head to the side. "What else?"

"There... may be a motive, and I'm afraid it only makes things worse for him." She wiped a stray tear from her face.

"What?" Melanie clasped her mother's free hand.

"Ronald Cartwright was married to Luther's daughter."

Bianca knew that much. "We did a search last night. She was the woman in an argument I saw at Bello Italian, where Lamar and I had dinner. But what else?"

"Well..." Deborah continued. "Luther told the police that he was trying to reconnect with her. Her marriage was over with Ronald, but he'd tracked her down and followed her here to Edenville."

"Luther killed Ronald to protect his daughter," Melanie replied.

Is that what the police suspect? Was she there? Had she been to visit her father at the hospital? The police must have questioned her by now. Still, that didn't change the powerful motive for Luther.

"Has she been here?" Bianca wondered.

Her mother said, "Yes."

"Why didn't you say so before?" Melanie asked.

Deborah waved her question away with her hand. "I was getting to that. A lot's happened in the last twenty-four hours." She exhaled a deep breath. "She didn't stay long, but she came. Not to mention, her relationship with Luther isn't the best, but they're working on it. The poor dear. She told me she hadn't been to a hospital since... losing her mother."

Bianca blew out her cheeks, releasing a deep breath. Her mother feeling frazzled was understandable. "I'm still having a hard time believing Luther did this."

Her mother faced her. "I never encouraged you getting involved in police matters before, but, Bianca, I have to now. You've got a knack for this."

What? Her mother wanted her to find the actual killer?

"I'm not asking you to put your life in danger, but if you find out something, *anything,* to help Luther, I'd appreciate it." Her mother's red eyes focused on hers with intensity. "I can't... Bianca, my heart can't take another loss like I experienced with your father. If there's anything you can do, please help Luther." She grabbed the heart pendant around her neck. "He told me this was his mother's... and he..."

Bianca's lips parted. A sharp pain went through her chest. Bianca recalled the nights she'd wake up from a nightmare, only to hear her mother crying over the loss of her beloved father. Bianca wished she could have done something then. What if now was her chance? She'd be careful. Alyssa was out of harm's way this time around. While facing another killer wasn't her first instinct, she wanted to help her mother.

"I'll see what I can do," Bianca said.

Her mother gave a faint smile. "Thank you. I still want you to be discreet. I won't want anything happening to you, either."

Melanie interjected. "Mom, I know you care for Luther, and I'm not saying he's guilty, but... don't you think—"

"He's innocent, Melanie. Sure, he has things in his past he doesn't like to talk about. Who doesn't? But I'm not abandoning him. Not when he needs me the most. Luther's a good man. I don't know why the evidence is stacking against him, but it's not true." There was conviction in her voice.

Bianca hoped her mother was right. How she prayed her mother was right. Her mother deceived by a killer was the last thing she wanted.

Chapter 8

Bianca walked down the hallway back to Luther's hospital room. Melanie had volunteered to ride with their mother to her house so she could change clothes and check on her dogs, Jasper and Horas, who were with a dog sitter. Realizing her mother wasn't comfortable leaving Luther alone, Bianca volunteered to sit with him. Not her typical Sunday, which usually included a family meal followed by relaxation, but she desired to support her mother.

She couldn't deny the plea in her voice. Deborah Wallace wanted her to help prove Luther's innocence. How? Where would Bianca start?

She bypassed an empty chair left in the hallway, listening to the slap of her heels against the linoleum floor. When she spotted Officer Butler, she squared her shoulders.

He stood to his feet. "Can I help you?"

"My mother had to leave, but she'll be back. I told her I would sit with Mr. Burkes," she replied.

Officer Butler raised a thick eyebrow, shifting his head from Bianca to the door beside him. When he nodded, she reached for the door handle.

"Thank you." Bianca was greeted by the scent of hand sanitizer when she opened the door. The door clicked behind her, but thankfully, it didn't wake Luther. Plain beige walls surrounded her, and she moved to sit on the plastic chair beside his bed.

He had a finger clip attached the index finger on his left hand. With his head turned to the side, she spotted a bandage on the back of his head. She didn't blame the EMTs for wanting him to stay overnight at the hospital. Head injuries could get worse without warning.

Bianca looped her purse on the back of her chair and placed her hands inside her lap. When Luther moaned, she scooted closer.

"De... De... Deborah," he whispered.

Bianca smiled, happy to hear him say her mother's name. "She's not here." She kept her voice low, not wanting to startle him.

Luther's eyes fluttered opened, and he turned to face her. "Bianca?"

"Mom will be back soon. How are you feeling?" she asked.

"Like I got hit in the head." He chuckled, but regretted it. He used his free hand to cup his furrowed forehead. "If only this headache would go away. They already gave me something for it, but when will it kick in?"

"Hopefully soon." Bianca swallowed, wondering where to start with her questions. "Do you... remember anything?"

His hand roamed from his head to the gray scruff on his face. Then he finally rested it on his chest. "I told the police everything." His eyes focused on her. "Are you all right?"

"Yes," Bianca said. For the time being.

Luther released a deep breath. "I guess it was coming, eventually."

She tilted her head to the side. Would he tell her more? "What do you mean by that?"

"Ronald. He... used to be my son-in-law. They didn't invite me to the wedding since Camille and I weren't... on speaking terms then," he explained. "I wasn't aware they'd divorced until she finally returned my call."

"You reached out?" Bianca's heart squeezed, witnessing him grip a fistful of his hospital gown at his chest. What kind of pain was he in?

"I did. She blamed me for her mother's death. When I left her mother, the grief took a toll on Norma, my ex-wife. I did things I'm not proud of, but when I saw the results of my actions, I wanted to change. I wanted Camille back in my life. Her and Lucy. Lucy's my granddaughter. She's around your Alyssa's age."

"Has Camille been here to see you?"

Luther's lips parted for a moment, but then he finally answered. "Yes. She stopped by last night."

Bianca needed to understand, so she asked the next question. "Why was Ronald at your car wash?"

Luther cleared his throat. "Camille told me he'd followed her here to Edenville. He begged her to see him, so she went to dinner with him, trying to give him the benefit of the doubt. He got riled up, and the restaurant made him leave."

That added up to what Bianca and Lamar had witnessed at the Bello Italian.

"I told her the next time Ronald reached out to her, call me. I told him if he didn't leave Camille alone, I'd... I... He'd deal with me."

"What?" Had he said what Bianca thought he'd said?

"I said he would *deal with me*." Luther squeezed his eyes shut. "But I didn't kill him. We struggled. Yes... I had my gun. Shots were fired, but no one was hit. Somehow, he hit me and grabbed my hand with the gun. Unfortunately, my old age kicked in and I guess he knocked me out. That's when I hit my head. I can only assume he took my gun. When I woke up, you were there. My gun was still in my hand, and... Ronald was... dead. I didn't shoot him."

Bianca sat back in her seat. The police had a motive to charge Luther with murder. There'd been an altercation, and with the gun in his hands, they had his prints on the murder weapon. "Did anyone else have a grudge against Ronald?" What if Camille had had something to do with it? How far would she have gone to protect herself from her ex-husband? Why frame her father, though? Resentment of the past and how he'd treated her mother?

"Camille's not a killer," Luther said. His protective, fatherly tone taking over. "She wouldn't do such a thing."

That's what Bianca had assumed about Priscilla Davis. Too chic to be a murderer, but she'd stabbed her own husband with a butcher knife. "Where's Camille staying? With you?"

"No, she's in a hotel."

Bianca reached out and touched his wrist. She was certain the police had talked to Camille. "I'm sorry this is happening. I'm sure the police will find out the truth."

Luther gave her a faint smile.

"I guess you'll want to postpone the fundraiser, right?"

"No." His eyes turned serious. "That's too important. I don't care if I'm in the hospital. Whatever your design plan was, go with it. I've seen your work, so I trust your judgment. If I... can't make it, you can work with Isaac."

Isaac? He didn't appear to be a fan of Luther's, either. Was their relationship always so cold? "But don't you—"

He clasped her hand. "This is too important, Bianca. A lot of veterans depend on the funds we bring in. I can't... let them down. No matter *what* happens."

Bianca's chest loosened. Either Luther Burkes was a changed man or he was a liar. She prayed he was the former.

"WHAT DID HE SAY?" MELANIE asked.

Once her sister had returned to the hospital with her mother, they agreed to leave, putting Officer Butler at ease. How long had he been on duty? Perhaps he was getting restless, waiting for another officer to replace him. Despite Officer Butler's less-than-chipper attitude, Bianca and Melanie said *goodbye* to Luther and hugged their mother. The sisters walked arm in arm down the hallway to the hospital entrance.

"He said he got into a fight with Ronald," Bianca answered.

"What else?"

"His daughter is staying at a hotel. He told her if Ronald bothered her again, he would deal with it."

A groan escaped Melanie's mouth. "Well, this just keeps getting better." She unhooked her arm from Bianca's. "I know you don't think he did it, but what do we really know about this man?"

Bianca raised an eyebrow. "Weren't you the one who was excited about mom dating again?"

Melanie huffed. "Not if her boyfriend is a *murderer*." Exhaling, her shoulders slumped as she faced her sister. "I don't want Mom to get hurt. She's been through enough already. I'm glad if she's happy, but... what if it's all an act?"

Bianca's lips parted. Melanie's words were practical. She didn't want her mother to be involved with a killer, either. Even if Luther was guilty, wasn't defending his daughter honorable? Self-defense, even if Ronald had attacked him.

"What are you thinking?" her sister asked.

"Why don't we... pay a visit to Luther's daughter?" Bianca suggested.

"We don't know where she's staying unless she's at the..." Melanie countered.

"The Stargaze Hotel," Bianca finished her sentence for her.

Melanie motioned down her dress. "Can we stop by the house and change first?"

Bianca unlocked the car and slid into the driver's seat. She cranked the engine and once her sister was inside, Melanie turned on the air conditioning. Pulling out of the hospital parking lot, she turned against the incoming traffic.

"Do you think she'll talk to us?" Melanie asked.

"I hope so. I'm sure the police have reached out to her by now." Bianca stopped at a red light. "I had a thought, but it's farfetched."

"What?"

"What if... Camille killed Ronald? Luther said she'd agreed to talk to her ex, and that's why Lamar and I saw her with him at the restaurant. She looked so terrified and she seemed to breathe easier when the servers had him leave. What will a woman do to protect herself and her child from a man like that?"

"A murder by a woman scorned?" Melanie added. "But if she killed him, why blame Luther? What did he do that would drive her to frame him?"

Bianca drove through the green light. "He wasn't a good husband to her mother. Perhaps there's still some bad blood between them, even though he's trying to make amends. Maybe's she's resentful? Bitter. Hates men overall. So, she kills her ex-husband and then blames her father out of spite."

Melanie tucked a loose curl behind her ear. "It makes sense, but we don't have proof."

"True. I can't tell that to Lamar without concrete evidence."

Melanie ticked off one finger at a time. "So the suspects we have are Luther, his daughter, and... who else? Who else would want him in jail?"

Bianca intended to find out. Not too long after, they pulled into the driveway of her house and she hit the remote to the garage. She'd pick up Casper later. He was in excellent hands with the dog sitter.

She unclicked her seatbelt. "Let's make this quick. We don't want to miss her in case she's not there. You know the front desk won't give us any info."

"True." Melanie undid her seatbelt and followed her sister inside their house.

Once Bianca was in her bedroom alone, she dashed to her closet, tossing her cell phone and purse on her bed. She settled for a cool sundress since the temperature had increased from eighty to ninety degrees. Flat shoes were easier to get around in and as she slipped them on, her phone ringing caught her attention. Was it her mother?

Rushing to the phone on her queen-sized bed, she saw Lamar's name flash on the screen. Did he have more questions about the case? Was this... a personal call?

"Hey," she greeted after releasing a deep breath.

"Are you busy? You sound out of breath."

"No, I'm fine." She sat on the edge of her mattress. "Melanie and I... just came from visiting my mother and Luther at the hospital."

No reply. Would he ask her if she was prying into police business?

"Is your mother all right?" he finally asked.

"She's... holding up as best she can, but..."

"But what?"

"This situation is... triggering for her. It reminds her of losing my dad," she explained, ignoring the twinge in her chest.

Lamar sighed. "I'm sorry to hear that, Bianca."

"Me too." The tightness in her chest loosened. "Any updates?"

"Nothing yet. Do you remember something else?" he wondered.

If only she did. Had someone else been there, and she hadn't noticed? Then again, she'd been wrapped up with Lamar on the phone. "No, and I'm sure my theories don't interest you."

"Not unless it's backed by evidence." His tone turned softer. "I was on a break and wanted to hear your voice, Bianca."

"That's sweet." Her chest fluttered. "And nice to know you're thinking of me."

"You'd be surprised how *often* I think of you, Bianca," he said.

Bianca did her best not to slide to the floor. Why did his voice dropping make her nerve endings stir? "There you go, flirting with me again."

He laughed. "Are you complaining?"

"No," she said.

Melanie tapped on her door. "You ready?"

"Yeah," she said, motioning her to leave.

Melanie wiggled her eyebrows, stepping back into the hallway.

"Yeah what?" Lamar asked.

"Nothing. That was Melanie. We're heading out for a bit." She didn't say more than that.

"Okay. Cool," he said. "Have fun with your sister. If I need anything from you about the case, I'll ask."

She dabbed at her forehead. "That's fine."

"And if I need anything else outside of the case, I'll tell you that, too," he added.

She giggled, despite her nervousness. Would she always react like a silly schoolgirl around him? "Thank you for that."

"Bye, Bianca."

"Bye." The phone beeped, alerting her the call had ended.

"Ready now?" Melanie asked once more, a smirk dancing across her lips.

Bianca narrowed her eyes at her little sister.

Chapter 9

Hopefully, she's here.

Bianca cut the engine to her Kia Soul and unclicked her seatbelt. A few cars crowded The Stargaze Hotel parking lot, but she found a parking space close to the entrance.

"Did you see what she was driving?" Melanie asked.

Being on a date with Lamar distracted her, but she was positive she could spot Camille. She hardly forgot a face. "No, I didn't." She kept the part about being distracted on her date to herself.

"Well, let's go." Melanie got out the car, followed by Bianca.

They entered the automated doors and stepped into the lobby. No one was at the marble-covered front desk, so Bianca took a seat in one of their cushioned chairs.

"What's the plan?" her sister asked.

"Not sure." They couldn't just ask the front desk for Camille's room number, and it wasn't as if they were family and the receptionist could call Camille's room to alert her to their arrival. Bianca tapped her foot on the tiled floor. *Ping.* The sound of the elevator opening.

An older woman, no older than her late fifties or early sixties, entered the hallway. Slender, bouncy salt-pepper hair, and thick eyebrows. She made eye contact with Bianca, but only nodded her head in acknowledgement.

Melanie glanced between her sister and the older woman. "You know her?"

"I don't think so."

The woman walked past them and through the automated doors. Perhaps she was new in town? Visiting relatives nearby? Bianca returned her attention to looking for Luther's daughter.

When another young woman emerged from the hallway, Bianca's lips parted.

She tapped Melanie's arm next to her. "That's her."

"Are you sure?" Melanie leaned in and whispered.

"I'm positive." Bianca stood. Would Camille talk to them? How had she reacted to her ex-husband's killing? With her hair in a low ponytail, pink yoga pants, white sneakers, and a fitted T-shirt, Camille rung the bell at the front desk. She dabbed her face with a towel. She must have just used the hotel's gym.

Camille huffed. "Where is everyone?"

"Yes, can I help you?" A woman with a pixie haircut emerged from the back.

Camille forced a smile. "Yes, thank you. Something's wrong with the TV in the gym. There's static coming through it and the picture keeps cutting in and out. I was hoping to watch as I worked out."

"Oh, no." The woman grabbed the phone in front of her. "I'll send someone to fix it right away. Thank you."

"Of course," Camille said.

"We can't just stand here, sis," Melanie said in a sing-song tone.

Bianca had a thought. Did she have a mock copy of Luther's flier inside her purse? Undoing the zipper, Bianca did an inward cheer at the cream folded paper. She took it in her hand. "Follow my lead. We're going to the dining area." Hopefully, this worked.

"Okay." Melanie fell in step beside her.

Bianca unfolded the flier as she walked. "I sure hope Luther's fundraiser at the car wash doesn't get canceled. He's worked so hard to organize this for the veterans in town," Bianca said, making sure Camille was in earshot.

Melanie followed along. "Yeah, it's too bad what happened."

In her peripheral vision, Bianca saw Camille turn her head, as if curious. She continued. "Who was that man, anyway? He wasn't a regular in our town. I hope the police can clear it up. I don't like seeing Luther go through this."

Bianca sat at a round table in the dining area. Melanie sat on the opposite side.

"Do you think she'll take the bait?" Melanie wondered.

Bianca kept the flier in her hands. Would Camille? She had no reason to tell them anything. Bianca didn't even know if Camille and Luther fully reconciled. Even if they'd reconnected, that didn't mean they'd repaired their relationship overnight.

"Excuse me." Camille approached their table. "Did you say, 'Luther's car wash'?"

Bingo. Bianca smiled. "Yes. Do you know the owner?"

Camille stiffened and crossed her arms. "He's... my father." She didn't sound too happy about that.

Melanie pulled up a chair for her. "Please, have a seat for a moment."

Camille hesitated, thumbing at her right ear. "I don't want to intrude."

Bianca waved her comment away. "Trust me, you're not. Your father's... actually dating our mother."

Camille's eyes widened as she sat down in between them. "You're Deborah Wallace's daughters. I didn't plan to meet you like this."

"You met her at the hospital?" Bianca asked.

"Briefly last night," Camille said. "My dad told me she had two daughters and a granddaughter."

"I'm the one with the daughter," Bianca said, raising her hand. "I'm Bianca Wallace, and this is my younger sister, Melanie." The women took turns shaking hands.

Camille gave a faint smile. "I have a daughter too."

"Is she here?" Melanie overlooked the dining area.

Camille shook her head. "No, but she'll join me this weekend. She stayed with some family on my mother's side for the early part of this summer. Her father and I..."

"Luther told me about your ex-husband," Bianca said. Not to mention his murder was the biggest news at the moment in Edenville.

A mirthless laugh escaped Camille's mouth. "Ronald. Humph! He wasn't much of a husband." Using the towel around her neck, she wiped at her damp eyes. "I was stupid to think he'd change."

Bianca knew that feeling thanks to her own past marriage. It had taken her a while to accept Malcom moving on with his new wife, Hope. She thought they could make it work if they tried again. She'd been wrong. Bianca blinked, not wanting to get sidetracked from the situation at hand.

"I talked to him," Camille continued. "He wanted to know where Lucy was and I told him I didn't feel comfortable with him being around her until I saw a genuine change in him. He got angry as usual." She sniffled. "The restaurant asked him to leave.

Whatever hope I had died way before he did." She touched a hand to her cheek. "I'm sorry. Why am I spilling my guts out like this?"

"I understand," Bianca said. "I'm divorced too, so I know the feeling of just wanting to vent. It's a lot to carry, but I can't imagine being in your position with him being..."

"Murdered," Camille whispered. "The police said someone shot him and... my father is the number one suspect." She used her towel again to wipe at her cheeks, but Bianca spotted a slight tremor with her hands.

"Who would have wanted to kill him?" Melanie asked.

"He said he wouldn't let anything happen to me, but I...," Camille whispered. "We've been trying to patch things up, my father and I. But... when trust is broken, it's hard to get it back."

Was she talking about Luther?

Camille exhaled. "I told the police Ronald was bad news, but I didn't kill him. My dad warned me about him, but I was still bitter over how he treated my mother, so I didn't listen. We were already in a terrible place, and my marriage drove us further apart. When I came to my senses, I left Ronald. I hated for my father to be right. He *always* has to be right. I guess he means well now. He said if Ronald did anything to hurt me, he would take care of it." Camille's fingers dug into her towel.

So far, her story matched Luther's. Bianca scooted the flier on the table closer to Camille. "You two have a past, but this town loves your father. Despite what's happening, he still wants this fundraiser to go on for the veterans."

Camille released the grip on her towel and held the corners of the flier. "I guess... he has changed. He wasn't around much when I was young. It's hard not to compare him now to who he was back then. My mother... tried *everything* to make him happy, but he..." Camille dropped the paper back on the table.

Melanie touched a hand to her shoulder. "I'm so sorry."

Camille's eyes blinked rapidly, and she licked her lips.

Was there more to her story than what she'd told them? Bianca didn't want to pry. Perhaps Camille needed a moment to gather her thoughts.

"I'm sorry. This is a lot to take in. I have to go." Her chair scraped the floor when she stood to stand. "I wish we could have met under better circumstances. Nice meeting you both."

"Nice to meet you too," Bianca said.

Melanie added. "We hope to see you again soon."

Camille gave a faint smile before she disappeared into the hallway.

Bianca opened her mouth to speak to her sister, only to hear a baritone voice outside the dining area.

"Camille? Camille?" a man called out.

"Oh, Bruce," Camille said.

Both Melanie and Bianca stood from their chairs. They took care to use the large plants to hide their snooping, but noticed Camille hugging a Caucasian man. He stood no taller than 5'10". In fact, when they broke their embrace, Bianca blinked. He favored... Ronald Cartwright. Did the man have a twin? Were they fraternal?

"This just got interesting," Bianca whispered.

"What?" Melanie said, keeping her voice low too.

"Are you all right?" Bruce asked, cupping Camille's face in his large hands.

Camille lowered her head, her neck appearing to shrink. "Your brother is..."

"I saw it on the news. I came as soon as I could. Is Lucy with you?"

"No."

He grabbed her hand. "Let's talk in your room." He led her to the elevator. "What floor are you on?"

"Three," Camille said.

That was the last thing Bianca heard. She straightened, rubbing her own neck as she backed away from the large plant. "So Ronald had a brother."

"And he seems close to Camille, too. He held her pretty tightly."

"Weird." Bianca returned to her chair in the dining area. "Did he show up in our Google search?"

Melanie answered. "I didn't see him. Perhaps Ronald is the most famous."

Bianca rubbed at her temples. "This doesn't help Luther. Camille and Luther both admitted Luther had said he would take care of Ronald for her." She ticked off her fingers. "Luther and Ronald had an argument. Luther had the gun when I found him. He had a motive, but I've got a nagging feeling something is... missing."

Melanie's face softened. "Is the truth staring us in the face, Bianca? It seems the more we learn about Luther, the more it only proves his guilt. Even if he's cleaned up his act now, that doesn't change his past."

"Mom thinks he's innocent," Bianca said. She never doubted her mother's judge of character. No one was perfect. Who was Bianca to judge if Luther owned up to his mistakes and changed?

Melanie sighed. "I just don't want us trying to prove he's innocent, and it turns out we're... wrong. Mom's in love, so of course he can't do wrong in her eyes."

Bianca's brow furrowed. "You think our mother is that gullible?"

Melanie closed her eyes for a moment. Then she stared at her sister. "I'm not saying I don't want to help, but we can't let that cloud our judgment. We're dealing with *facts* here, Bianca."

"Now you sound like Detective Sims." Bianca rubbed at her head. "It just feels to me like..."

"Like what?"

"Like Luther's being set up. Why allow himself to get caught if he'd killed a man? Why not wear gloves to hide his prints or stash the body somewhere else?" Bianca gasped. "I wonder if it's still there."

"What are you talking about?" Melanie's nose wrinkled.

"The wristwatch." Bianca grabbed the flier and her purse. "When Lamar and I went to the creek, I think I spotted a watch on the ground."

"And whose was it?"

"I don't know, but I'm wondering if I saw something important without realizing it. I couldn't tell what type of watch it was, but it looked expensive. It makes me wonder if there're any more clues out there." Bianca hurried out the dining area to the hotel entrance with Melanie at her heels.

"That makes little sense. You found Ronald's body at the car wash."

Bianca snapped her fingers. "And I didn't see another car. How did he get there?" Luther himself drove a silver GMC truck.

Melanie's eyes widened. "Oh, no. Bianca, do you mean...?"

"What if the killer murdered Ronald beforehand and dumped the body with Luther?"

"And Luther lied about it? Why would he tell the police he fought with Ronald in the car wash if he didn't?"

They slid back into Bianca's car. She started the engine. "It *does* make him seem guiltier. That doesn't make sense. Unless... he's protecting someone."

"Like his daughter," Melanie said. She rested her head against the headrest. "She seemed a little... shifty. Her hands were shaking as she spoke to us, unless it's just because she's in shock about everything going on."

"I noticed that too," Bianca said. "And... it wouldn't surprise me if there's more to her story. Hopefully, she told the police everything."

"I don't know how you come up with these theories," Melanie added. "You think we'll find something at the creek?"

"We need proof. It's a long shot, but something's missing from this case. And Camille didn't say where she was yesterday when it happened."

"I don't think we asked. Why would she volunteer that information?"

Bianca pulled out of the parking lot. "She volunteered everything else, didn't she?"

Melanie sighed, clicking her seatbelt. "Well, we need to get Casper first."

Bianca smiled. "Even better. His sense of smell will come in handy today."

Chapter 10

B ark. Bark. Bark.

Casper stood on his hind legs in Melanie's lap as Bianca drove them to the creek. What would they find there? Was her gut feeling a long shot? How far back had the police looked into Ronald Cartwright's whereabouts?

Melanie rubbed Casper's back. "Did you notice anything about Ronald's clothes besides the bullet hole?"

Bianca turned onto the gravel road, approaching Edenville's creek. "I can't remember. There was a lot to digest after seeing him." Thinking back, she pictured Ronald's body. He'd been face down on the ground and shot in the back. The soap water from the car wash had soaked his dark jacket.

Bianca's eyebrows furrowed. Had there been mud on his shoes? Grass remnants on his clothes? The sleeves on his jacket had fit so well, she couldn't tell if he'd been wearing a wristwatch. Yet an important man in real estate... how could he not wear one?

Parking her car, she cut the engine. Melanie held Casper close and secured his leash. They didn't want him to wander off. Stepping out of the car, Bianca kept her phone handy while Melanie held on to Casper's leash. His collar jingled as he scratched behind his ears.

"Where are we looking for?" Melanie asked.

Bianca moved forward, trying to retrace her steps. Lamar had walked her to her car. The gravel crunched around her as she walked, with Casper and Melanie following her. "I think perhaps somewhere here." Birds splashing in the water filled her ears as the leaves and pine needle fragments drifted along the sun-dappled surface. When the sun reflected on a shiny object, Bianca inched closer.

"Is that it?" her sister asked.

Bianca knelt down. Mud fragments speckled the face, but it still ticked, showing the correct time. Melanie knelt down next to her as Casper sniffed the air.

"I think so. I'm not sure if it belonged to him." Opening a browser tab on her phone, Bianca searched for Ronald Cartwright's name. Surely there were more pictures of him. Had he worn a wristwatch in public? Bianca spotted a photo of him at what appeared to be an awards dinner.

The picture dated two years prior, but Camille was present in the photo in a floor-length ivory gown next to Ronald in a black-and-white tuxedo. He was stoic, and her smile appeared forced, but Bianca recognized something on his left wrist. She was certain the wristwatch's face looked the same.

"Mel?"

Her sister stared at the photo and back to the ground. "It looks the same."

"If only we were sure." Bianca grabbed a hair pin securing a curl behind her ear.

"What are you doing?"

"If my hunch is correct..." She used the pin to turn it over. Would there be an engraving? Would it show the name of the person if it had been a gift? Bianca's lips parted. *For Ronald.*

"Oh, boy." Melanie held on to Casper's leash as he dug his paws into the ground. "We should call Detective Sims."

Bianca agreed. Though his chances of being irritated with her were high, she couldn't hide this from him. He could rule out the evidence even if it wasn't Ronald's. Straightening to her feet, she called his number.

"Hey, how are you?" he asked.

"Hey, I'm at the creek we were at this past weekend," she said. "Do you remember asking me if something was wrong before I went home?"

"Sure. Why?"

"Lamar, I think I found Ronald Cartwright's wristwatch. It's still here."

Silence.

"Lamar?"

He sighed. "Are you alone?"

"No, Melanie is with me," she replied.

"Atkins and I will be there soon. Get in your car and lock the door until we get there," he said. Then he hung up.

"Well?" her sister asked.

Bianca gestured to the car. Melanie picked up Casper, and they walked back to sit inside the car. Bianca locked the doors as requested.

"What did he say?" Melanie placed Casper in the back seat.

"He didn't. He and Atkins are on their way."

"Was he... annoyed?"

"Maybe, but if I'm right, he'll understand."

Melanie's mouth quirked up, but she stared ahead. "If that's Ronald's wristwatch, what was he doing here?"

"Or whom was he meeting here?" Bianca countered. She cupped her forehead. "It makes no sense."

"What's your theory?" Melanie asked.

"He met with the killer here. Things turned ugly. They killed him here, dumped him at Luther's with no one seeing them. Then they pinned it on Luther."

Her sister shook her head. "That's what I don't get. Why him? Who has a vendetta against Luther?"

"Perhaps they're not from this town." Bianca stared at her sister. "It's possible Camille is capable of murder. Even Priscilla surprised me when she killed Martin."

Melanie blew out her cheeks. "None of us imagined that coming. We attended her dinner parties. I didn't figure she… was capable of something like that."

"Sometimes, it's obvious, and other times, it's not." Bianca tapped a finger on her lips. "But if Ronald has a brother, I wonder if he knows something. He's close enough to Camille to come check on her. I wonder if the police have talked to him yet."

Gravel crunched behind them, and Bianca spotted a familiar police car. Lamar stepped out first, followed by Detective Atkins.

Bianca unlocked the door. Melanie grabbed Casper, holding him in her arms this time.

"Ladies," Detective Atkins greeted. His trimmed goatee complemented his dark brown skin, and his stocky built showed he put long hours in the gym.

Lamar said, "Melanie. Bianca." Then his eyes roamed about the trees and forest trails made by the animals.

Bianca saw his jaw clench. Lamar would keep things professional, but he would tell her to go home and let the police handle the investigation. She pointed to the area she'd seen the wristwatch. "I saw it here." She led the way, with the group following her. Then she unlocked her phone, ready to show the picture of Ronald wearing it. "I didn't touch it, but there's an engraving on the back."

Detective Atkins knelt down. He put latex gloves on his hands and pulled out a small plastic bag. He picked up the wristwatch, dusting off the dried mud. When a phone rang, Melanie gasped.

She dug into her back pocket while keeping Casper secure in her other arm. "Sorry. I have to take this." She returned to the car, taking Casper with her.

Bianca folded her arms over her chest.

"And you're saying you saw it this past Friday night?" Lamar asked.

"Yes, Detective," she replied, keeping it professional. "I figured someone lost it. It's not uncommon, but then..." She unfolded her arms and held up her phone. "I found this." She zoomed in closer.

Lamar stood closer, and she did her best to ignore his woodsy cologne. His eyes shifted back and forth. He faced Atkins. "What do you think?"

Atkins said, "It's possible. We can run it to the lab and have it tested. We didn't find a watch on the body, but there was an imprint on his left wrist implying he'd worn something."

Lamar exhaled. "Call it in. If the crime took place here, we should search the area."

Bianca didn't say a word.

Atkins nodded, placed the wristwatch in the small plastic bag with his gloved hands. Then he headed back to the police car.

"Looks like I'll be here awhile." Then he stared at her and gestured to her car. "You can head home."

She nodded. "Do you... at least want me to send you the picture?"

"Go ahead."

She tapped his name on her phone and sent the photo as an attachment.

His phone pinged. "Thank you. Do you remember anything from that night?"

"No. I have a theory, but... I don't think you'll want to hear it." She swallowed despite her dry mouth.

Lamar's demeanor stilled, aiding in his observation. "Indulge me, Bianca."

"What if... the killer murdered Ronald here? There's hardly anyone here after dark. What if they shot him here, and they dumped his body at Luther's car wash?" she explained.

"For what purpose? Do you have a suspect? A motive?"

Bianca's right hand played with her stud earring. "No, but if that's Ronald's..." She paused. "Unless someone took and dropped it without him knowing."

He pinched the bridge of his nose. "I admit, Bianca, you're clever. You're smart and you've come in handy in these last couple of cases, but I don't want you getting close to another killer." His face slackened. "Someone kidnapped you not too long ago. I... want *nothing* like that happening again."

Bianca's skin shivered despite the warm day. Held at gunpoint and forced into Hunter Graham's car wasn't her best memory. She'd even shot off a gun to get him to stop the car. "I'm sorry. I was only trying to—"

Lamar took her hand in his, turning his back to the cars behind them. Bianca stared into his gray eyes.

"It's different now, Bianca. You're not just another citizen, I swore to protect as an officer. You're more to me than that. *Much more.*" His eyes beamed with sincerity.

Goosebumps slid along the back of Bianca's neck. "Thank you for telling me."

"You're welcome." He released her hand. "I realize it's in you to help. I can't force you to stay out of anything, but I need you to promise me something."

"What?"

"Call me if something comes up. Don't handle things yourself," he said. "Some things are out of your control, but try."

Bianca clutched her phone in her hands. "I don't want you to worry about me. I'll be careful."

He gave her a soft smile. "I know you can take care of yourself, too."

"Thank you."

When she heard police sirens approaching, she figured his backup had arrived to search the grounds.

"I need to get back to work." He stepped back. "Go home. Rest. Check on your mom."

Bianca agreed. "Okay."

He backed away and met with the other officers. Atkins joined the huddle as Lamar gave directions. Bianca joined her sister back inside her car.

"Are they going to check out the watch?" Melanie asked.

"Yeah. They're going to see if it's a match. Ronald wasn't wearing one when they found him, but..." She touched her own left wrist. "There was an imprint implying something was there."

Melanie blinked. "Whoa."

Bianca stared in the backseat, spotting Casper gnawing on his Dalmatian chew toy. "He wants us to head home." Bianca cranked the engine. "Who was it who called you?"

Melanie didn't reply. Instead, she clicked on her seatbelt.

"Mel?" Bianca repeated. "Was it serious?"

"Oh, no." She waved away her question. "It was... Jordan."

Bianca's lips parted. Melanie didn't confirm if they were exclusive, but the two liked each other. "Oh, really?"

Her sister glanced at Bianca momentarily, then looked away. She wrung her fingers together and shifted in her seat. "Bianca, don't start. Besides, we're parked in what could be a crime scene, so I don't want to discuss my personal life here."

"No problem." Bianca put the car in reverse. "We'll just discuss it at home."

"What about you and Detective Sims? I saw him take your hand," Melanie teased.

Screech! Bianca slammed on the brakes in response, only to have Detective Atkins and Lamar snap their heads to stare at her. Casper barked. *Great.* Bianca rolled down her window. "It's fine. My foot slipped. Nothing's wrong."

They both nodded in reply, and Lamar waved goodbye.

Bianca forced a smile, pressing her lips together tightly. Melanie giggled.

Chapter 11

Bianca blew out her cheeks, tossing her keys into the basket once she and Melanie had arrived home with Casper. Not the Sunday she'd expected, but she hoped Lamar and Detective Atkins found more answers at the creek. She'd wanted to explore the place herself, but his stern rejection of that prospect with just strong eye contact with her changed her mind.

His words made her chest flutter. He was right. Things were changing between them. While Bianca enjoyed spending time with Lamar, she wasn't sure how far they would go. That would unfold with time. For now, she wanted to enjoy the chemistry between them.

When he took her hand, her skin tingled. It felt the same way when he'd held her hand on their date that past Friday evening. Bianca ran her thumb over her palm. She missed his touch already.

Melanie plopped on the couch after unhooking Casper's leash. "What a day."

Bianca plopped next to her.

"Do you suppose they'll find anything else out there?" her sister asked.

"Not sure." She rubbed at her head. "I wish I had an idea where to search further, but..."

Melanie raised in her seat.

"I understood what Mom said at the hospital, and I want to help, but—"

Melanie shifted in her seat to face her. "But what?"

"Lamar... Things are... This differs from the times before. It's..."

"You're dating a detective, Bianca," her sister finished her sentence.

"Right. He told me how he felt when Hunter had kidnapped me." Bianca shivered. "I can still remember being scared myself. The gun in his hand, driving me out of town... I don't blame him for being worried."

"I was worried too," Melanie added. "I'm just glad both you and Alyssa came home safely." A chuckle escaped her mouth. "It wasn't funny at the time, but when I told Detective Sims that Hunter had kidnapped you, his nostrils flared. He called Detective Atkins for backup. It didn't take him long to catch up with you."

Bianca smiled. "He... came after me."

Her sister returned the gesture. "He's a good one. I'm happy you're giving it a chance."

Bianca folded her arms, raising an eyebrow at her little sister.

Melanie blinked. "What?"

"So... Jordan called you?"

Melanie's mouth twisted. "Uh-huh?"

Bianca flung her hands in the air. "It's not like it's a secret, Mel."

Her sister groaned. "I know, but like you, I'm getting used to it. It has been awhile for me, too. It's not like eligible bachelors have been lining up outside our door."

"Only because we told Mom to take our names out of her database," Bianca joked.

They both laughed.

"True. She said, 'I can't call myself the best matchmaker in town and have two single daughters.' She's something else." Melanie arched her eyebrows.

Bianca tilted her head. "So... you and Jordan?"

"We're trying it out. There's no rush, so we're seeing how things go. Spending time with each other."

Bianca held back her squeal.

Melanie rolled her eyes, sensing her excitement. "Go ahead."

Bianca shrieked and hugged her sister, wrapping her arms around her neck. "I knew it!"

"Jordan's sweet. Handsome, but he carried a torch for Nicole for so long," Melanie said.

Bianca pulled back and faced her sister. "Yeah. He took it hard when she met Chad."

Melanie wrung her fingers together. "We talked about that, too. It wasn't a heavy conversation, but we wanted to be sure if we were both ready."

"What did he say?" Bianca wondered. "If you don't mind me asking."

Melanie exhaled. "While he cared about her, he realized Chad was the man she chose. He wanted her happy, even if it wasn't with him." She touched a hand to her chest. "It warmed my heart to hear that from him. Though it hurt him when she married someone else, he wasn't bitter."

Bianca smiled, proud of her friend for doing an honorable thing.

"Do you have plans for later? Maybe checking on Mom again at the hospital with Luther?" Melanie asked, standing to her feet.

"I'll call her." She narrowed her eyes at her. "Do *you* have plans?"

Melanie's eyes sparkled with apparent excitement. "Jordan's picking me up. He won't tell me where we're going, so it's a *spontaneous date*, as he calls it."

Casper trotted over from his water bowl and stood on his hind legs in front of Bianca. She picked him up, and he rested in her lap. "I guess it's just Casper and me tonight. I have work to do, anyway. Luther's fundraiser is this week. Not to mention the Summer Festival."

Melanie's lips parted as if to respond.

"I know, but despite what's going on, Luther doesn't want the fundraiser to suffer," Bianca explained. "There are veterans in town depending on it."

Melanie raised her hands in a gesture of surrender. When the doorbell rang, she scurried to her room. "He's here already. Stall!"

Casper barked and jumped from Bianca's lap to the floor. She answered the door. Jordan stood in a plaid shirt with his sleeves rolled to his elbows, dark jeans, and white sneakers. As usual, he greeted her with a bear hug, picking her off the floor.

"How are you?" he asked.

Bianca patted his back. "Okay for now." When he placed her on her feet, she pinched his arm.

Jordan rubbed at his skin, though she doubted she'd bruised his toned body. "What was that for?"

She gestured to the hallway. "You and Melanie."

He walked inside, and she closed the door behind him. He knelt to pet Casper, who licked his hand. "She told you?"

"Yes, but I can't imagine why *my friend* since college didn't give me a hint." She folded her arms, but she wasn't angry with him. Her lips upturned.

Jordan straightened to his feet. "It was too soon to tell, Bianca, and you're protective of her. I didn't want to say anything until I was sure I wanted to pursue her."

Bianca rubbed at her elbows. "I understand. You're a man of your word. Mel will be safe with you."

"How's your mom?" he asked.

Bianca walked to the couch, and he joined her. "We saw her earlier today. I'll call her later to make sure she gets some rest. She doesn't want to leave Luther's side."

Jordan leaned forward and rested his elbows on his thighs. "I can't believe it myself." He looked at her. "And you found the body?"

"Yes."

A *tsk* escaped his lips. "How do you do it, Bianca?"

She bristled. "It's not like I plan for these things to happen."

"Just be careful." He reached for her hand. "I may date your sister, but I care about you, too. You're my friend."

Bianca accepted the gesture. "You're a good friend too."

"Okay. I'm ready." Melanie emerged from the hallway, having changed from her jeans to a white sundress decorated with small yellow sunflowers. "I couldn't decide between earrings."

Flushing at the sight of his date, Jordan released Bianca's hand and stood to his feet. "You... you're beautiful."

Melanie secured the back of her round stud emerald earring. "Thank you." Then she eyeballed him. "You don't look too bad, either." As Bianca tried to leave the room, Jordan sauntered to Melanie and kissed her cheek. She giggled and touched his stubble-covered face. Casper barked, interrupting their moment.

"I guess he can't stand the mushiness, either," Bianca joked.

"Ha ha," Melanie countered. "I'll see you later, okay?"

Bianca waved. "Have fun. I'll be here working or watching reruns."

Jordan chuckled, taking Melanie's hand. "See you later, Bianca."

The couple exited the door with Casper at their heels. Bianca locked the door behind them as Casper scratched at the base. She leaned against the door, smiling. *Melanie and Jordan hitting it off...* her smile grew wider. Then Bianca walked to her home office with her dog following.

DESIRING A BREAK FROM work, Bianca took Casper on a walk to the park. A Sunday walk would take her mind off things for a while, but she would check on her mother and Luther before calling it a day. Thank goodness an overcast sky shielded her from the scorching sun.

A cool breeze sighed through the trees as Bianca inhaled the scent of flowering plants. Kids laughed and yelled as they played on the nearby swings with their parents calling out to them. She passed the pond and the gazebo, choosing a nearby bench to sit on. Since the park rules permitted it, she unclasped Casper's leash and let him roam about.

Despite her intentions to forget about Ronald's murder case, she wondered if Lamar and Detective Atkins had found anything else at the creek. Had anybody seen anything, and they hadn't come forward? If Ronald was there, who was with him? If Camille was to blame, had she had help? Who else possibly transported Ronald's body to the car wash?

Casper barked at a butterfly, jumping on his legs while trying to catch it. Bianca giggled at his antics and took out her phone. She didn't think Lamar would talk to her about the case, but if he had further questions, he'd call her.

"I'll stay as long as you need me to," a man's voice said. It came from behind her as she sat on the bench.

Bianca wasn't one to snoop on other conversations, but if a person was talking out loud, what did they expect? She couldn't tune out everything. Instead, Bianca opened up a browser window to her online website, monitoring Casper.

"You're welcome. Did the police leave?" the man asked.

Police? Bianca leaned back in her seat.

The man continued. "Don't worry, Camille. This will all be over soon."

Bianca blinked as her lips parted. Camille? Was this the man she and Melanie had seen with Luther's daughter earlier? What was his name again? *Bruce*, if she remembered correctly.

"I told you I'll take care of things. Don't worry," Bruce added.

Bianca's skin crawled. If only she could decipher Camille's words, but the volume was too low.

"If you do what I tell you, nothing's going to happen," he said.

Bianca held back her gasp. Her eyes shifted to Casper, who was digging a hole next to a flower bed. Pulling her lips in, Bianca exited the browser and headed straight to Lamar in her contacts.

Do you know Ronald had a brother? Sent.

Her knee bounced. He had to have known if they were at the Stargaze Hotel. Unless Bruce had left before, Lamar had had the chance to question him. Her phone buzzed.

Bianca????

She imagined his deep voice now. He'd probably been covering his face once he'd seen her message.

Do you know he had a brother?

We talked to him already. He wasn't in town during the murder.

Can he confirm that? He's here at the park now on the phone with Camille. He promised to 'take care of things.'

Bianca, we're working on it. If his alibi checks out, there's nothing we can do. You're not questioning him, are you?

"I'm heading back there now." Bruce stood from his seat on the bench and walked to the parking area.

Bianca's eyes followed him. Calling out to Casper, she hoped she could get a license plate number to keep an eye out on Bruce personally. If Lamar looked into it, he would have already had it. Securing Casper's leash once more, her eyes searched for Bruce. A couple walked past her hand in hand and she smiled, while she spotted another couple pushing a baby stroller.

Where had Bruce gone that quickly? Bianca took a few steps ahead, hoping he hadn't already pulled off from the parking lot. Moving from the grass to the gravel, she traced her thumb over Casper's leash in her hand. Then she heard indistinct muttering.

Bianca inched closer, wishing the ground didn't crunch under her sandaled feet. Casper sniffed around, pushing a loose rock with his paw.

"Stop worrying, all right?" Bruce said.

Bianca tucked herself between two pickup trucks, noticing Bruce rested a hand on top of a black Honda. Opening a browser window on her phone, she Google searched for Honda and matched the car. A Honda Civic Si Coupe. It couldn't have been older than a 2010 model based on the images she compared it to. Then she exited the window, returned to her camera feature and zoomed in. Despite her diagonal location, she could get the license plate number.

Bruce got into his car and cranked the engine. Bianca saw him pull off, his tires sputtering loose gravel in his haste. Where was he going?

Buzz. Buzz. Bianca saw Lamar's name on her screen. Returning to the park, she answered. "Yes?"

"You didn't answer my last message," he said, sounding less-than-pleasant.

"I didn't question him. Besides, he's gone," she told him.

He sighed. "Why do I feel there's more than what you're telling me now?"

Bianca bit her bottom lip.

"Bianca?"

"I got his license plate. I don't know whom he was talking to on his phone after his call with Camille, but it sounded suspicious."

"Bianca, the truth will come out if something is going on. I thought I asked you to be careful?"

She returned to her park bench. Casper stretched and scratched behind his ears. "I came to the park to walk with Casper. Can I help it? The guy sat behind me talking out loud."

"Guess not," he said.

"I *am* being careful," she reassured him.

"I believe you."

"Any word on the watch? Does it belong to Ronald Cartwright?" she asked, scooting to the edge of the park bench. Then she thought better of it. "If you can't tell me, I understand."

"I need to return to work, Bianca," he answered. "If I need anything from you about the case, I'll ask."

"Okay."

He hung up and Bianca placed her phone in her lap.

Casper barked.

"Okay," she said. "One last walk around before heading home?" The only thing that crossed her mind was that if she kept pushing it, this case would drive a wedge between her and Lamar. Would she be able to step aside if it came to that? It was too soon to tell.

Chapter 12

Fallen acorns from the trees and squirrels both intrigued Casper as he and Bianca walked along the nature trail in the park. She hadn't been down the dirt path since Pricilla had had someone stalking her. Though it hadn't been humorous then, Bianca recalled falling into the pond with Lamar and how he'd kept her from hitting her head on a rock. How he had protected her then, never mentioning his feelings for her.

When had things changed? Had he always liked her? She would have to ask for fun. Casper pulled her along, alerting Bianca she was walking too slowly for him. She indulged her pup and picked up the pace. As they circled the dirt path, Bianca paused, only to detect an older woman bent over as if she were looking for something.

"Oh, dear," she said, her voice a resounding alto.

Bianca waved to her. "Can I help you? Did you lose something?"

"Oh!" The older woman straightened, and she pressed a hand to her chest. No taller than five foot seven, with deep blue eyes and a few fine lines around her mouth.

Bianca held up her free hand. "I'm sorry. I didn't mean to scare you."

Casper barked and wagged his tail.

The woman waved off her comment with a smile. "That's all right, dear. I didn't see you coming. I lost the back to my earring and I can't seem to find it." She waved around her. "I've looked everywhere. I've had these earrings for so long, they don't hold like they used to."

Bianca focused her eyes on the ground. "Is it silver? Gold?"

"Sterling silver," the woman said.

When Bianca spotted something small and silver on the ground, she pointed to it. "Is this it?"

The woman came to her side. She picked it up, releasing a sigh of relief. "Thank you so much." When she straightened, Bianca focused her eyes again on her medium length salt-pepper hair.

"I've seen you before." She snapped her fingers to help jog her memory. "At the hotel. The Stargaze Hotel?" They'd made eye contact briefly.

The woman's eyes widened. "Yes, you and another woman were by the front desk."

"That's my younger sister." Bianca extended her hand. "By the way, I'm Bianca Wallace."

The woman chuckled. "Forgive my manners. I'm Susan Hayward, like the movie actress." She took Bianca's hand to shake.

Bianca's grin grew, observing an old, almost half-moon looking scar on the woman's hand. The old line was long enough to notice, but her name took her aback. "No kidding."

"It's true." The woman pulled her hand back. "Though I don't know how to act to save my life, I'm honored to be named after an amazing woman. Are you a fan of the classics by chance?" She motioned to the trail, and they walked along with Casper. He didn't seem to mind the unfamiliar face, so he didn't bark.

"I watch them now and then." Bianca pressed her lips together. "Since you're named after a classic Hollywood star, have you seen all her movies?"

"A few, but I can't say which one's my favorite," Susan replied.

Bianca asked, "So what brings you to town? Are you new to Edenville or are you visiting?"

"Visiting," she replied. "So, what do you do? I'm a retired jeweler."

Bianca's eyes widened. "Wow! Did you own your own business or worked for a larger company?"

Susan said, "I started my business after my first marriage ended. Over the years, I created pieces, but never made it big. I sold my business to another jeweler once I recognized I couldn't carry it by myself anymore." She pointed to her earrings. "One of my first creations. I made necklaces and bracelets, too."

Bianca snapped her fingers. "I could have done your graphics. I'm sure you would have made it big in this town."

"You're a graphic designer? I love to meet creative people. I'd love to see your designs sometime," Susan said. "Well, now I'm traveling and taking advantage of retirement and enjoying life. I saw the quaint town and thought, why not?"

Bianca suggested. "If you're staying until the weekend, we have some exciting events you can't miss. We have a summer festival and a car wash to raise funds for our veterans in town."

Susan nodded, tapping a slender, manicured finger to her thin lips. "I heard about the fundraiser. Is it true what they're saying in town? The man hosting this fundraiser... killed someone?"

Bianca's lips parted at a loss for words. "The police are searching for the truth."

"It's sad, really."

"It is. I know the man, so it's hard to witness this," Bianca said, thinking more about her mother.

"Are the police sure he didn't do it?" Susan asked, facing her with a raised eyebrow.

"I believe he's innocent. Luther Burkes is a respected man in this town," Bianca added. She didn't want to disclose too much information, since she'd only met this woman. If town gossip was already spreading, she couldn't blame Susan's curiosity.

"I've known my share of men people *respected*." Her eyes focused on Bianca. "They only disappoint you. They say the right things and the mask comes off. Then you discover the truth about them." She touched her cheek as if to re-center herself. "I'm sorry. What did you say his name was?"

Bianca repeated. "Luther Burkes."

"Ah," Susan said. "Well, I hope true justice prevails. Crime shouldn't go unpunished."

Bianca parted her lips to respond, but Susan rubbed her hands together.

"It was nice meeting you, Bianca." She touched a hand to her shoulder. "It was great talking to you and I hope I can stay long enough for the events." Then she pointed to her earring with her scarred hand. "Thanks for all your help."

Bianca smiled. "You're welcome. I hope you enjoy your visit here."

Susan waved goodbye, and Casper barked after her. Bianca bent to pet him, giving him the attention he obviously wanted.

"She seemed... nice," she said.

Casper barked again.

"You don't think so?" She tilted her head to her dog.

His tongue hung out.

"Right, you can't tell me, anyway." She giggled, scratching behind his ears. "We're done for the day. Let's go home."

Chapter 13

Casper sprinted to his chew toy once he and Bianca had returned home from the park. After a long day, she wanted to crash on the couch. Grab a bowl of homemade popcorn and watch a movie. Action and adventure film or a romantic comedy? Either way, perhaps that would take her mind off the recent murder in Edenville. Still, it had been a few hours, and she wanted to check on her mother.

Sitting on the couch, she went to her favorites in her contacts. Deborah Wallace picked up on the first ring.

"Mom?" Bianca sat back on her couch, resting a foot on her coffee table.

"Hi, sweetie." Her mother didn't sound chipper. She sounded worried, and even if she didn't voice it, Bianca picked up on it.

"How's Luther? Can he go home?" She was sure his head injury wasn't too severe, but she understood the doctors taking precautions.

Her mother sniffled. "No, the... police still suspect him. It's possible they'll arrest him on suspicion of murder. His prints are on file. There's a motive. And it's not as if someone else has come forward."

Though not surprised, Bianca hoped something would surface, proving Luther's innocence. "How are you? I'm sure this is... tough."

"I'm doing my best. It's hard to go through this again, but... as it was with your father, I believe Luther is innocent."

Bianca rubbed at her neck. How would they clean up this mess? Perhaps Bianca should return to the crime scene. Sure, the police had taped it off, but what if returning jogged her memory? Though true, the least likely people could be responsible for heinous crimes, Bianca didn't see that with Luther Burkes.

The man was a gentleman to her mother. Generous to the community of Edenville. Even if he had a past, wasn't he making amends for it? His daughter had reached out. His granddaughter would arrive that weekend. Weren't things turning around for Luther? Who would sabotage that for him?

"The hospital will discharge him soon. Then it's up to the police," her mother continued.

"Is he cooperating with them?" Bianca asked. Did Luther contact a lawyer just in case?

Her mother paused.

"What, Mom?"

"I... I feel he's leaving something out. Suppose there's more to the story than he told the police."

"What makes you say that?"

"Detective Atkins came back. They found a wristwatch they suspect belongs to this Ronald guy at the creek. Luther denied knowing anything about the watch. Why would Luther go to the creek, anyway?" her mother wondered.

That was what Bianca wanted to understand. So the watch belonged to Ronald. Though that wouldn't prove that someone else was involved? Either Ronald dropped it there outside of the crime, someone brought the watch there without Ronald to begin with, or Luther himself killed him there and brought him back to the car wash. The watch didn't prove Luther's innocence at all. "Mom, did Luther work all day yesterday?"

Her mother released a deep breath. "Yes."

That had to count for something, sort of, if her creek theory was correct. How long had Ronald been dead to begin with? Bianca raked her fingers through her hair. There was Camille. Bruce. Luther. Who had the stronger motive? "Mom, has Luther shown genuine interest in reconnecting with his daughter?"

"Yes. Why?" she asked, sounding curious.

"How far would he go to... protect her?"

"He's her father, so I'm sure he would..." Her mother gasped. "Bianca?"

"Mel and I met Camille today. She's staying at the Stargaze Hotel. We talked some before she left. This whole topic disturbed her, Mom." Bianca expected nothing less. Being too calm would have been weird.

"I never pictured this. Our Sundays are usually church and family dinners," her mother added.

Bianca moved her foot from the coffee table to the floor. Perhaps Bruce and Camille had worked together? They seemed close. If in desperation Camille had killed Ronald, was Luther protecting her by covering for her? How far would he go to repair his relationship with his daughter? When Bianca heard muffled voices in the background, her mother cleared her throat.

"I need to go," her mother said. "I'll call you later."

"Okay, Mom. Love you."

"Love you."

They hung up. Shifting her head, she found Casper gnawing on another chew toy. At least this case wasn't bothering *him*. Standing to her feet, Bianca paced to her kitchen. It was just her for dinner, and while she'd enjoyed Judy's taco casserole earlier, Melanie and her mother must have taken it home when they left to get their mother a change of clothes.

Opening the refrigerator, Bianca searched for leftovers, but her stomach quivered. She had the same information as the police. Was she being gullible? Melanie didn't find it hard to believe Luther's possible guilt, but Bianca wasn't certain.

Buzz. Buzz. She closed the refrigerator and returned to her phone on the couch. She didn't recognize the number. Curious, however, Bianca answered. If it was a solicitor, she could always hang up and block the number.

"Hello?"

"Bianca Wallace?" a tenor voice asked.

"Who's calling?" No sense in telling her identity too soon.

"This is Isaac Murphy," he said.

"Oh, right," Bianca said, feeling relieved. "I didn't recognize the number."

"A lot's happened. I'm calling because Mr. Burkes has me taking over until the... police find out what happened."

Bianca asked. "Do you know what happened? Did you see—?"

"No." He barked, only to sigh. "I'm sorry. This... has me on edge."

No kidding. He didn't seem too happy talking about Luther either at Richard and Judy's restaurant. "You don't think Luther's guilty... do you?"

Isaac answered. "The man saved my life, but it's not like he's the image of perfection." He huffed. "Sure, I fell into a toxic crowd when I was younger. Luther was the only one to give me a job afterwards, but... why am I telling you this?"

"It's okay." Bianca hoped he'd say more. "I'm curious. What if he's being framed?"

"It's not like his daughter's been around. He didn't go into detail since we're not that close, but Camille shut him out. Bitter about how things had ended with him and her mother. I think she knew, though, that despite their estranged relationship, he'd do anything for her still. When she called Luther while he was at work earlier yesterday..."

"She did?" Bianca was on the edge of her seat.

"Yeah. She kept going on and on about her ex-husband. How she wouldn't let him get away with it. I didn't hear what. I only heard in passing and Mr. Burkes' volume was up on his phone. Ms. Wallace, I'm sorry. I didn't mean to dump that on you. That wasn't why I called."

"Don't apologize. This took everyone by surprise," she reassured him.

"Anyway, the fundraiser is set for this Saturday. Can you send over the fliers no later than Wednesday?" he asked. "The police promised it would be open in time for the car wash. I just hope people still show, despite a... dead body being found here."

Bianca hoped so, too. "The cause is enough for people. Was there anything else you needed?"

"No, thank you. I'll take care of the rest. Mr. Burkes wants nothing to interfere with the car wash. So, I'm doing everything I can to make it happen," Isaac said.

"That's very kind of you to keep it going."

"It's my job." He cleared his throat. "Anyway, you enjoy the rest of your evening."

"You too. Thank you." He hung up without another word, and Bianca clutched her phone to her chest. There wasn't much information to go on, but Isaac suspected Camille too. But how well did he know her if she never came around? Then again, if Luther had talked about her enough, Isaac must have made his own conclusions about the man's daughter.

She showed in town after years of estrangement. Had it truly been to make amends, or had there been another motive? Then her ex-husband followed her. How had he found her? Private investigator, perhaps? Did Luther know?

Ding dong. Casper barked and sprinted to the door. Bianca checked the time. Eight o'clock in the evening. She wasn't expecting anyone, and Melanie had a key, so she wouldn't have rung the doorbell.

She walked to the entryway but looked out her small window first. Bianca blinked. Lamar. He wasn't with Detective Atkins, so was this a personal call? She answered.

He pivoted to face her. His jacket was off and his collar unbuttoned. "Hey."

"You're not working?" she said.

"Finished for the day." He held up a plastic white takeout bag. "Dinner on me?"

Bianca smiled. "Are you sneaking in another date with me?"

He walked inside and her heart skipped since he was only a breath away from her lips. He closed the front door behind him with his foot.

"Not sneaking. I'm asking. Would you like to have dinner?"

Bianca swallowed. "Depends. I can be a picky eater."

He chuckled. "From R&J's, Chicken Alfredo. Though they usually close early on the weekends... I asked Judy to make an exception. When I told her it was for you, she obliged happily."

Bianca's lips parted at his thoughtfulness and her friend's generosity. She ignored the lightness in her chest. "Sounds good." Judy never disappointed anyone with her homemade Alfredo sauce. "I accept." Then she turned to face the back door. "How about on the porch outside?" She almost never ate out there, but the sky was clear and a cool breeze would top off the occasion.

Lamar walked past her. "I'll meet you out there." Casper followed him. "Want to come?" he asked the dog. Casper barked, wagging his tail.

Bianca grabbed glasses, napkins, and a pitcher of iced tea. She turned on the porch light, and by the time she'd joined Lamar, he had her patio table set for them to eat.

He pulled out her chair. "Here you go."

Bianca set the glasses, napkins, and the pitcher on the table, taking a few trips to do so without dropping anything. Casper ran around the yard, completely ignoring them as he sniffed around the fence. Bianca sat in her seat, realizing Lamar must have moved the patio chairs closer together. She hoped she could get through dinner without sounding like a bumbling teenager. "Thank you. What made you think of this?"

He poured her a glass of tea along with his. Then he sat next to her. "I was on my way home and wanted takeout. Then... I wondered if you'd like dinner."

"How did you know I'd be alone?" she asked, undoing the plastic silverware.

He smiled. "I didn't. I had it all planned in my head how to ask your sister for some privacy."

Bianca giggled. "Well, it worked out, since she's on a date with Jordan."

"They're official?"

Bianca shrugged. "I don't know, but they're giving dating a try."

"Good for them," he said.

She sipped from her chilled glass. "I appreciate this. It's... sweet and thoughtful of you."

He winked at her. "You're welcome."

Bianca took a bite from her meal, needing something to do. They ate for a few minutes in silence, but it wasn't awkward. While she appreciated pleasant and meaningful conversations, she always wanted a comfortable silence with someone. Bianca felt overwhelmed in a good way. Sometimes, simply being with a person surpassed everything else.

"Your mother okay?" he asked.

Bianca nodded. "I checked on her. I hope she can get some rest." She set her fork down.

"You want to ask me something?" he said.

"No, I don't... want to ruin the evening," she said. "I know how you feel about me getting involved with police business."

He exhaled. "You're not ruining anything, Bianca." He turned in his chair to face her. "I'm not angry, but I won't lie and say I don't worry. I told you earlier... Things are different."

Before Bianca realized what she was doing, she touched a hand to his stubble chin. The small hairs pricked at her fingers, but the sensation danced up her arm. Lamar turned his head, leaning into her touch. He kissed the inside of her palm. Bianca's lips parted, her nerve endings stirred.

"Yes..." she whispered. "Things are different now."

This time, his hand reached out, and he cupped her cheek. Bianca's breath quickened. If a simple touch did this, how would she act during a kiss? Her gaze dropped to his lips. How would he kiss her? Would it be hungry and demanding or tender? Which did she prefer?

She hadn't been kissed since... Malcom. For a time, he'd been the only man in the world for her. Sadly, that ended. Now, in front of her, was something new. Despite her quivery, twitchy muscles, she wanted to explore. All she had to do was leap and face her fears.

Her hand ran down Lamar's cheek, traveling to the back of his neck.

"Remember what I told you?" he asked.

"You wouldn't kiss me until I was ready," she whispered. His voice made her shiver. She inched closer.

He moved closer, too. "Bianca..." Why did her name sound so angelic when he said it?

His woodsy cologne seeped into her nose. Tilting her head, Bianca closed her eyes.

Buzz. Buzz. Buzz. Buzz.

Lamar groaned. "No way."

Bianca giggled, despite her own frustration. She rested her head on his shoulder.

"I'm sorry I have to take this," he said.

Bianca pulled back. "I understand. Go ahead." She sat back in her seat and took a long gulp of iced tea.

Chapter 14

"Everything okay?" Bianca asked, as Casper stood on his hind legs, begging to be scratched behind his ears. She obliged him with a smile.

Lamar hung up his phone, resting his arm to his side. "Yeah."

Had he gotten a call about the case? Had something else come up to incriminate Luther Burkes? "Are you sure? You look worried."

He returned to his seat next to her. "I'm good, but I may stop by the crime scene on the way home. There was an anonymous tip about someone hanging around the car wash."

Bianca gasped.

He must have noted her reaction. "What, Bianca?" He pointed to her with his index finger. "What's that look?"

She scratched behind Casper's ears as he rested his head on her thigh. "Well... I had the same idea."

"To what?"

"Go... back to the crime scene."

Lamar sat back in his chair with a sigh. "Bianca..."

"Just listen." She stopped petting her dog to face him. "If you're going, why can't I go with you? Don't forget, I'm a witness, so something can jog my memory. I was in shock myself, so it's possible."

He bit the inside of his cheek. "You're very persistent."

She gave a faint smile. "I won't deny it. We can even bring Casper. Put his sense of smell to good use."

Casper barked.

Lamar smiled. "I'm not staying long. Just need to check up on something."

"We'll leave when you're ready, unless... I see something important. If I do, will you promise to hear me out?" she asked.

Lamar sat up, close to her. "I don't mind hearing you out, Bianca, but I can't solve a case on theories."

"I know," she said.

He pinched the bridge of his nose. "All right. But only because you're a witness. If you see something that helps the case, I don't mind." He stared at the table. "We can go after we clean up."

Bianca's smile grew bigger and Casper followed her inside as she transferred the glasses to the sink to wash. With Lamar's help, they cleaned up in no time at all. After grabbing her phone, Casper's leash, and her purse, they headed to Lamar's car.

The drive to Luther's car wash didn't take long, and once Lamar had parked, Bianca secured Casper's leash around his neck. His collar jingled as he fell in step with Bianca. Flashes of yesterday evening danced in her mind once more, but she approached the crime scene, though yellow tape blocked it off.

Casper sniffed around her, but Bianca paused her steps in the same place she'd stood the former night. Her eyes drifted to the corner. She hadn't spotted Luther passed out on the ground. Then her eyes shifted to where she'd found Ronald's body. She observed a few dark spots on the concrete, marking where his blood had spilled.

No doubt the police had searched the area. What else could she pick up on that they hadn't detected?

Bark. Bark. Casper wanted to walk around, and judging by the way he tugged on his leash, Bianca wasn't moving fast enough for him.

"Everything okay?" Lamar asked.

"Yeah. Just going to walk around a bit." She let Casper lead the way. They bypassed the garbage bins, and Bianca's nose wrinkled at the stench. "Maybe there's nothing here." While she wanted to help on account of her mother, what if he wasn't innocent? Even if he wasn't the killer, what if he'd been involved?

Luther told her he would take care of Ronald for Camille. Walking back to find Lamar, Bianca spotted something on the ground. It shined because of the fluorescent lighting, and she bent to inspect it. A small stud earring? Whom did it belong to?

"Lamar?" she called out.

He didn't waste time sprinting to her side. "What's wrong?"

She pointed to the stud earring. "I found this. I don't know who it belongs to, but..." Bianca fiddled with her own stainless steel heart earrings. She wore small earrings occasionally.

Lamar took out a small plastic from his jacket pocket. Picking it up with his gloved hands, he held it in the air. Round black stud. "I don't remember seeing this." He dropped it inside the bag. "Any customer could have dropped it without knowing. Unless... someone else came after we swept the place... and dropped it. Mr. Burkes doesn't have security cameras, though I think it'd be a smart investment now."

Bianca didn't say a word, but she agreed. "I don't remember seeing anyone else here. I parked in the front unless..." She straightened on her feet.

Lamar followed. "Unless what?"

"They parked in the back."

Lamar's eyebrow raised and when he jogged to the back, Bianca followed with Casper, who apparently enjoyed the run. When she caught up to him, he stood with his hands at his hips.

"Atkins looked back here." He bit at his bottom lip.

Bianca took out her phone to use her flashlight. Nothing but wet concrete, but the earring was something. Casper tugged at his leash, directing Bianca closer to Detective Sims. Lamar had his own flashlight, illuminating the spot in front of him.

"Anything?" Bianca asked.

"No, I can send a few officers out here tomorrow, but this proves nothing."

Bianca bobbed her head, tapping her foot to the concrete.

"Let's head back to the front." Lamar gestured for her to follow him, and she did, along with Casper.

"Can I ask an honest question?" she asked.

"Sure," he said.

"Are you going to arrest Luther?" She stopped in her tracks.

Lamar blew out his cheeks. "Bianca, all I can tell you is the evidence against him is steep."

Bianca opened her mouth to reply, but something in the shadows behind the main building caught her eye. "Lamar?"

He blinked. "What?"

"Is someone else here?" she whispered.

He pivoted and looked behind him. He held his hand up to her. "Don't move." Reaching for the gun on his hip, he grabbed it without hesitation.

Bianca's scalp prickled. Who else was here? The car wash was closed. Unless... had the killer returned to the scene of the crime, too? She focused her eyes ahead as Lamar inched forward, ready to shoot if need be. Bianca's breathing slowed.

"Bianca," Lamar whispered, and motioned for her to come closer.

She picked up Casper and sprinted ahead.

He gave her his car keys. "Get in the car. Now."

She didn't ask him why, but she hurried to the car. As soon as she closed the door, she saw Lamar dash ahead. He was chasing someone, but whom? Casper barked and Bianca scooted to the driver's seat from the passenger's side. The engine revved as she started it. Her eyes followed Lamar as he ran down the street. She didn't recognize who was in front of him, but she quickly put the car in drive and the tires screeched as she sped ahead.

Casper jumped, placing his feet on the dashboard. Lamar kept his pace with the person in front of him, and when he saw Bianca driving, he didn't stop. He'd probably lecture her later, but for now, she would catch up with his suspect. The person, tall, broad frame, dark pants and a hoodie, didn't head to the main street leading into downtown Edenville. Instead, the person headed onto a two-lane street. Bianca followed, speeding the speedometer to over seventy miles per hour.

Now ahead of the runner, she cut the person off, slamming the brakes. Thank goodness Lamar was close behind because he pinned the person to the ground. When cars beeped on the opposite side of traffic, Bianca pulled to the side of the road. She cut the engine, leaving a barking Casper inside Lamar's car.

She paused her steps, seeing Lamar handcuff the man face down on the ground. Lamar spoke into his walkie-talkie.

"I need backup on Elm Street," he said.

"I didn't do nothing!" a man's deep voice shouted.

Bianca knew that voice.

"You want to tell me what you were doing at an official crime scene?" Lamar asked.

"You got nothing on me!" he spat back.

"Isaac?" Bianca said, folding her arms over her chest. She could see his face clearer after he lifted his head.

"Ms. Wallace?" He appeared dazed.

Lamar helped him to his feet. "You know him?" he asked Bianca.

She nodded. "He's Luther's manager for the car wash."

Lamar looked at him. "Of course, we questioned you earlier today. Tell me what you were doing there."

Isaac stood a few inches shorter than Lamar. His dark jacket hid his tattoos, and the hoodie covered his round face well at night. He didn't reply to Lamar's question.

Bianca wondered the same thing. When she heard police sirens approaching, her breathing eased.

Chapter 15

"So what were you doing at the car wash after hours?" Detective Atkins asked.

Isaac bowed his head, his hands still cuffed behind his back. Bianca stared at him, wanting to know the same thing. He might have been checking the books as the manager. Maybe there were last-minute details for the fundraiser. Why run away, though? If he was innocent, why would he try to escape the police?

Isaac pressed his thin lips together.

"If you tell us, this will go a lot smoother for you," Detective Atkins replied.

Bianca clutched her phone in her hands. Even if Isaac had planned on working late on whatever, why keep quiet with the police? Or... was he involved in something else? Her mind pondered the reasons for his actions tonight.

"I'll take you home," Lamar said, touching the small of her back. He led her back to his truck.

Bianca ignored the shivers up her spine. "You're not staying to question him?"

"Atkins can fill me in. I need to get you home." When he opened the door for her, Bianca spotted Casper asleep in the passenger seat. She smiled and scooted him over, resting his head on her lap. "He's out for the night."

Lamar closed the door behind her and sprinted his way to the driver's seat. Once inside, he started the engine. "Where did you learn to drive like that?"

Bianca swallowed. "I've had some experience before." When she and Melanie investigated Martin Davis's murder, they were tailed. No sharp turns there, but she'd gone past the speed limit.

Lamar pulled back onto the two-lane road, bypassing the two police cars.

"Why did he run?" she asked.

Lamar didn't answer at first, but he finally said, "He wasn't expecting us."

"Where was his car? The parking lot was empty."

"He walks to work because he lives near the car wash."

Did he? Or did he perceive the police would track his car?

"We found cash on him," Lamar said. "More than most people carry around."

Bianca blinked. "That makes no sense. He said Luther's done nothing but help him. Why would he steal from the man?"

"I intend to find out." When they came to a red traffic light, he looked her way. "I wish I could keep you away from this, but I'm glad you were here."

"You kept up with him pretty well," she said.

"Why do you think I have to keep working out?" He gripped the steering wheel a bit tighter. "I hate it when suspects run, but that comes with the job, too."

Bianca sat back in her seat. Another theory crossed her mind. "Lamar?"

The light turned green, and he pulled forward. "Yeah?"

"If Isaac stole from Luther, do you imagine it's tied into the murder case?" she wondered.

He sighed. "Atkins will bring him in for formal questioning. This is nothing but a robbery."

They sat in a comfortable silence until he pulled into the driveway of her house. She didn't ask any further questions, and judging by the furrow in his brow, enough was on his mind.

"I have to admit... we worked well together tonight," he said. He turned to face her and his smile grew. "I thought you were going to run him over for a second."

Bianca giggled, rubbing Casper's back. "That didn't cross my mind. I was only trying to stop him."

To offer personal contact, he reached for her free hand. "And you did just that."

Bianca stared into his gray eyes, being cautiously optimistic. They'd been so close to kissing earlier until his phone had rung. "I guess... I should get inside. I have to wake up early for work."

"Same," he said, running his thumb over the top of her hand. "Thank you for your help tonight."

"You're welcome," she replied. Why was it hot all of a sudden?

He leaned over the console. "Perhaps on our next date, we *won't* get interrupted."

"So you're asking me out again? Did I impress you that much tonight?"

His smile grew. "Bianca, you impressed me way before tonight."

She opened her mouth to reply, but a charcoal Sedan pulled up beside them. Jordan and Melanie were back from their date. When her sister got out of the passenger seat, she squinted her eyes to look inside Lamar's tinted window.

"Detective Sims?" She saw her sister. "Bianca?"

"I better go." Bianca cradled Casper in her arms. His eyes fluttered opened at all the commotion.

"I'll see you later," Lamar said. He waved to her sister and Jordan.

Once Bianca had closed the passenger door behind her, Casper in hand, Lamar pulled out onto the street. When he drove off, he left Jordan and Melanie staring at Bianca.

"What?" she asked them both.

"You didn't tell me you were going out with Detective Sims tonight," Melanie said.

"I guess it wasn't just us having a date." Jordan smirked.

Bianca rolled her eyes. "It wasn't a date. Well... it *was* a date, but then it wasn't a date and then I stopped a thief while driving his car."

"Come again?" Melanie blinked.

"Um, okay, that sounds like quite an evening, but I have work tomorrow. I'll call you later." Jordan kissed Melanie's cheek. "Give me the details later." He patted Bianca on the back and slid into his driver's seat. Once Jordan had left, Melanie followed her sister back inside the house.

Bianca placed Casper back in his doggy bed, only to straighten to her feet to spot her sister eyeballing her.

"What happened tonight?" Melanie asked.

"Lamar came over and brought dinner." Bianca eased into the kitchen for a bottle of water.

"And...?" her sister coaxed her.

"Then he got a call and returned to check the crime scene again tonight," Bianca continued.

"And he took you with him?"

"I am a *witness*, Mel." Bianca took a gulp.

Her sister rubbed at her forehead. "Okay, so what's this about stopping a thief in his car?"

"You recall Luther's manager, Isaac?"

"Yes."

"He was there," Bianca said. "I saw something in the shadows and Lamar ran after him. He'd given me the keys to his car already, so I drove ahead and cut Isaac off on Elm Street."

Melanie walked to the living room and plopped on the couch. "Some night, I guess."

"And... Isaac had cash on him. I'm not sure why he would steal from Luther, but I'm guessing there's a connection to the murder."

Melanie sat up. "What does Lamar think?"

"He's not on board... yet," Bianca said.

Her sister rubbed absently at her own arms. "Why would Isaac steal from Luther?"

Bianca intended to find that out.

TIRED FROM A LONG DAY, Bianca crawled into her queen-sized bed. Though she rested her head on her plush pillow, her eyes wouldn't stay closed. She knew she had to wake up early. The new work week had started, but Isaac running from Lamar replayed in her mind. What was he hiding?

Sitting up in her bed, she glanced at her alarm clock. 11:45 p.m. and she couldn't fall asleep, so Bianca reached for her phone. She could use the internet and social media to find Isaac Murphy. Starting with Instagram, she typed in his name. Usually, people used their names as their handles, and profiles for other Isaac Murphy's popped on the screen. She spotted the dark-brown hair and light-brown skin of the Isaac she knew and clicked on his main profile.

He had a few photos of him at the gym while the rest showed him working on cars. Was he a mechanic on top of being Luther's manager? Did he need more income if he was running his own side business? Bianca raised her knees in bed, resting her phone against them as she scrolled further down his page. Nothing incriminating.

Looking upward at her ceiling fan momentarily, she decided to search Camille's name. She figured it was a long shot. Though Camille's handle included a few numbers, Bianca recognized her face. Clicking on her main page, Bianca checked her latest post. Two weeks ago, it was dated, and Camille was in front of a bridge.

The background of trees and foliage didn't look familiar to Bianca, so she scrolled further. Camille had a few pictures of her daughter, Lucy, who could have been her identical twin with her long hair and high cheekbones. Bianca wondered if she was getting anywhere until she stumbled on another post, dated a month prior. Camille stood with Bruce, with Lucy in between them.

Since Camille had tagged Bruce in the photos, Bianca went to his personal page. Not too many selfies. Mostly him making jewelry pieces. He made jewelry? Bianca didn't expect that, but the man had over fifty-thousand followers. She'd dig more into it later, so she returned to Camille's page, staring at the photo of her, her daughter, and Bruce.

Bianca thought nothing more of it. The post had more than one photo, so she scrolled to see another image. Only Bruce and Camille this time. Though Camille's eyes faced forward, Bruce's gaze remained on her. Bianca noticed while one hand was to his side, the other embraced Camille's waist. It looked higher than it ought to have been since a mid-waist side-grab was more common for friendly photos, unless... there was more between Bruce and Camille?

Bianca gasped, sitting up in bed, dropping her phone to her lap. Had Ronald been aware of this? Sure, he and Camille had divorced. Had he been trying to win her back, when he discovered she was with his brother? Then why would she have agreed to hear him out at Bello Italian if she'd moved on? Bianca blew out her cheeks, returning her phone to her nightstand. She had more questions than answers after tonight. Who'd killed Ronald Cartwright? Who'd had the strongest motive?

Chapter 16

Mondays were slow at the office, and Bianca didn't mind it at all. It gave her time to work in silence, distraction-free. Almost distraction-free. She recalled the photos she'd seen the night before of Camille and Bruce. Sure, he was her brother-in-law and every family dynamic was different, but the way he held her in the picture appeared too intimate.

Not to mention how he'd visited her and they'd gone upstairs to talk privately in her hotel room. Bianca sat back in her cushioned office chair. Her ideas from last night were returning. If Ronald had known something was going on between them, perhaps it set him off into a jealous rage.

Bianca perked up. Had that caused an argument? Bruce and Ronald fighting over Camille? Had Camille and Bruce worked together to get rid of Ronald so they could be together without interference? Would they have *murdered* him? The pieces fit, but was it a strong enough motive?

How did Luther fit into it all? There was no way he had played any willing part in it unless Melanie's suspicions were right. What if his "nice guy" routine was all an act to woo her mother? To get on their family's good side? What did he gain from that?

Bianca's timer went off on her phone, alerting her it was time for lunch. Good. A break well deserved. Locking up the office, she inspected the street. Orderly parked cars, dogs barking as their owners walked them, and a few brakes squealed as cars stopped at the nearby traffic light.

Wringing her hands together, Bianca made the short walk to R&J's Restaurant and Bakery. She wondered what the specialty meal was for today. The bell chimed when she entered the entryway, and thank goodness, the lunch crowd hadn't poured in yet. Her first thought was to take her order to go, but when she spotted a familiar woman at a nearby table, she blinked.

The park yesterday. Susan... something.

Susan raised her chin, putting down her copy of *Wuthering Heights*. "Hi." Then her eyes brightened. "From the park. Bianca. Right?"

Though her comments were kind of unusual, even somewhat rude during their last meeting, Bianca was gracious. "Right. And you're Susan..."

"Hayward." She giggled. "Don't worry. Some people mix it up with Hayworth."

"Like Rita?" Bianca said.

"You know your classics." She gestured for her to join her. "Please join me. Have you ordered yet?"

Bianca sat, looping her purse strap at the edge of the table next to the wall. "Not yet. I was wondering what the specialty meal was for today. I'm friends with the owners."

Susan pointed to her plate. "Lunch is Chicken Marsala. I rarely eat carbs for lunch, but I couldn't resist when the server told me about it."

Bianca's stomach growled. "That sounds delicious."

"I see you made it before it got too crowded," Judy said. She had pulled her red hair into a low tight bun and placed a chilled cup of iced water on the table for Bianca. "What will you have, friend?"

"The Chicken Marsala," Bianca answered.

"Perfect." Judy made a note on her pad and walked away.

"If you love her cooking, you'll love her desserts," Bianca added.

Susan waved her comment away with her scarred hand. "Don't tempt me." She pointed to her plate with her fork. "This is bad enough for my diet, anyway."

Bianca asked. "If you don't mind me asking, how did that happen?" Pointing to her scar.

"Swimming accident. Can you believe it? It's what I get for being *too* ambitious." She chuckled.

Bianca laughed. "Understandable. So... are you still liking Edenville?"

"I am. It's peaceful." Susan looked upward for a moment before returning eye contact. "It's good to have that."

"I agree," Bianca said. "My mom said the same thing. We lived in Atlanta when I was younger, but I think this place is her permanent home. Where are you from?"

Susan wiped the corners of her mouth. "North Texas, but I've been doing a lot of traveling. I have the means to do it, so I'm taking advantage of my free time."

"Do you wonder how the new owner is handling your business?" Bianca wondered what she would do once she retired.

"I check in now and then." Susan beamed. "Thankfully, he doesn't mind. He's even taken it further with a better online presence." She chuckled. "I tried to the last few years, but I never got into social media. So, I'm resting now." Then she touched her hand to her chest. Her fingers picked at her neck as if she was missing something. A necklace?

"Did you lose something?"

"Oh, nothing important. Anyway, that's my story and I'm enjoying my retirement."

Bianca didn't ask anymore. "I hope to do that one day. Enjoy the payoff for my hard work."

Susan said, "You can do that now. It doesn't take a lot of money. Simple things are what we need. You're young, dear. Use this time."

Bianca smiled. "I appreciate that. Thank you." Though there was one thing in particular she'd pondered pursuing, she wouldn't disclose that to a stranger.

The bell chimed again, and Bianca's breath hitched when Lamar and Detective Atkins walked inside. They must have been taking a lunch break too. She didn't mean to stare, but his dark-blue suit complemented his brown skin. His beard neatly trimmed, as always, and her fingers tingled when she'd touched his face the night before.

"Another *friend* of yours?" Susan asked her.

Bianca grabbed her cup of water. After taking a gulp, she answered. "Umm... yes."

Susan squinted her eyes. "Hmm... I think I see what you're implying. Don't worry, I won't say a word about it. Though I have heard that you two bumped heads a few times." She stared at the men as they ordered.

"Bumped heads?" Bianca's eyebrows squished together.

"I heard in passing that you've helped in a couple of police cases. Murder in this small town? I can't imagine."

No doubt Ms. Ella was her source. "Unfortunately, it happens here too, but..." She locked her gaze on Lamar. He threw his head back in laughter with Detective Atkins. "We have detectives who work hard to keep us safe."

Susan crossed her eyes as she observed the officers at the counter. "I don't blame you. He's handsome."

Bianca faced Susan once more, hoping she wasn't blushing. "Uh-huh."

Susan chuckled. "Having adventures doesn't always mean traveling. They could mean..." She looked back at Lamar. "Adventures of the heart."

Bianca had no reply. Her feelings had to be obvious for a stranger to notice.

Susan opened her purse and took out cash for her meal. "Tell her she can keep the change. I have to get going." She patted Bianca's hand. "Nice to see you again, Bianca."

"You too."

Susan walked out the door, the bell chiming behind her. Detective Sims—Lamar looked back, only to make eye contact with Bianca. He was on duty. He wouldn't waste time staring. He needed to return to work.

"Here you go," Judy said, setting a hot plate in front of Bianca.

"Can I get a to-go box?" She had to return to the office. No sense in staying and drooling over the officer.

Judy blinked. "Okay. I won't ask why, either." She winked at her, returning to the swinging doors.

Bianca dug into her purse for her wallet. Heat rushed to her face. They'd only started dating, and she didn't want to fall for him without really getting to know him first. This time would be different. She wasn't the wide-eyed high school girl who fell for charm alone anymore.

She was a businesswoman. Level-headed. Bianca even had a daughter to think about. She wouldn't sacrifice her daughter for a relationship. Bianca exhaled, calming her racing thoughts. It was too soon to tell. *Just enjoy the process.*

"Here you go." Judy set the Styrofoam box on the table, along with a white plastic bag.

"How much do I owe you?" Bianca asked.

"Actually… it's paid for," Judy said.

Bianca jerked her head back. "What? By whom?"

Judy directed her eyes to Lamar as he set his food tray across from Detective Atkins. Perks of a ready-made bakery. It could serve customers at tables or have dinner to-go, along with pastries.

Bianca's lips parted. She had intended to slip away with a wave. Now, she had to say *thank you.* "Thanks for telling me."

After taking Susan's cash and cleaning up her dirty dishes, Judy whispered, "I'll talk to you later." She returned to the counter to take another order.

Bianca used her fork to transfer her food from her plate to the Styrofoam box. She secured it inside the bag. Blowing out her cheeks, she grabbed her to-go plate and her purse and approached the men's table. "Gentlemen."

Detective Atkins smiled. "Ms. Wallace? Good to see you."

"Leaving so soon?" Lamar gestured to the seat next to him. "You can join us if you'd like."

"No thanks. I have to get back to work." She held her bag up. "Thank you for lunch, anyway."

"Anytime," Lamar replied.

Bianca almost melted like candle wax. What was it about his deep voice? "Enjoy your…" She spotted his lunch. "Salad." She moved to the door.

Pressing a hand to her head, she inhaled. She refused to look at him through the restaurant window. Bianca walked to the middle of the street, hoping Lamar wasn't staring after her either. Though her pulse raced at the notion. *SCREECH!* Bianca's head snapped as a car's engine roared. Rubber burned, followed by smoke as the car barreled straight toward Bianca, changing course to follow her as she moved.

"Watch out!" a woman yelled.

"Slow down!" a man's voice shouted.

"Help!" Bianca dashed for the sidewalk, but she wouldn't make it in time.

"Bianca!" Strong hands grabbed her, pulling her to safety back onto the sidewalk, swinging her lunch out of her hand onto the sidewalk. *SPLAT*! Spectators pointed to the car as it screeched around the corner. Chatter and murmurs increased along with the barking dogs. Bianca clung to her rescuer with her free arm, while her other hand gripped her purse. Lamar.

"It's okay," he whispered in her ear. "You're safe now. I'm here."

Gripping her purse strap, she trembled in his arms, resting her head on his shoulder.

Chapter 17

Bianca's fingers dug into Lamar's shoulder. What had happened? Someone had attempted to run her over? For what?

"Bianca?" Lamar waved a hand in front of her face. "Are you okay? Talk to me."

"I'm-I-What-Did that..." What was she supposed to say?

He led her back inside R&J's Restaurant and Bakery. Judy rushed to her side as soon as he'd opened the door. The bell jingled, and Bianca sat in an empty chair next to the window.

"What happened?" Judy asked.

"A car almost hit her," Lamar said. "Can you get her some water, please?"

Judy dashed to the back while the other patrons whispered among themselves. Some people stood in front of the window, thinking they could find something else outside.

"I'm fine." Sure, Bianca was a little dazed from the adrenaline rush, but no harm done. Probably a new reckless driver in town. Residents of Edenville rarely sped up that way on the main street downtown. Sped up? Bianca swallowed as Judy brought her another chilled glass of water.

"Take a few sips," Judy told her.

Bianca did. She also noticed Lamar's hand never left her shoulder.

"Thanks," she told Judy.

"Are you okay?" her friend asked. "Do I need to call your mother? Melanie?"

"No, that's okay. I'll be all right."

Judy didn't look convinced, but she didn't reply. Instead, she nodded to both Lamar and Bianca, returning to the counter to attend to her customers.

Detective Atkins came back through the front door. When had he come outside? Bianca took another sip. Too much had happened in the last few minutes.

"Anything?" Lamar asked him.

He shook his head. "It happened so fast, witnesses didn't get the license plate. They only saw a beige Buick."

Bianca choked.

Lamar patted her back as she coughed. "Maybe she needs to get checked out."

"I'm fine." She looked up at Detective Atkins. "What kind of car did you say?" She couldn't have gotten a good look at it, either. Too busy trying not to get killed.

"A beige Buick. That's what a few witnesses said outside," he replied.

Bianca's eyebrows squished together.

"What?" Lamar asked her.

"That sounds like the same car from yesterday," she said.

"You've seen it before?" Lamar took out his notepad from his back pocket.

"Melanie and I were on our way to the hospital to visit our mother and Luther. The car ran a red light and almost hit us."

Who was driving the car? Were they after her? Had it all been a coincidence?

"Had you seen this car prior to yesterday?" Detective Atkins asked.

"No," she said. "To be honest, I thought nothing more about it. People run red lights now and then. I was just glad they didn't hit us."

Lamar exhaled. "We'll see about finding who drove the car. In the meantime, I'm walking with you back to the office."

Bianca's eyes widened. "That's unnecessary. I'll be fine." The whole point of her leaving earlier had been to give herself some space from him.

"I insist." Then he looked at Atkins. "I'll meet you back at the station." He wasn't taking *no* for an answer.

Bianca, being too frazzled to argue with him, didn't deter him any further. She waved goodbye to Judy and exited the restaurant with Lamar after Judy replaced her lunch. Her previous plate was no good. Lamar touched Bianca's elbow and led her to walk on the sidewalk, while he walked closer to the street.

"Did you get to finish your lunch?" she asked.

"Don't worry about it." He looked over at her. "What matters is you're all right."

Bianca gave him a faint smile. "Thank you for saving me. It happened so fast, I froze for a moment." They paused in front of a red traffic light.

"You're welcome," he said. When the sign showed "walk," they proceeded.

"And..." Bianca said. "Thank you again for lunch." She held up the new plate. "I mean the first... you know what I mean."

"Why didn't you stay?" he asked.

She wouldn't tell him her reason. Not now. "I needed to get back to work."

"It's too bad I'm on the clock," Lamar said. "We could have had lunch together at your office. I don't think Atkins would have minded."

Bianca's grin grew wider. "He knows?"

"I haven't exactly kept my feelings a secret, Bianca. He figured it out, especially when Hunter took you," he explained.

Bianca's jaw slackened as her mouth cracked open.

Lamar cleared his throat. "Here we are."

Bianca distracted herself by looking for her office keys inside her purse after handing Lamar her food to hold. "Thank you for walking with me. I can take it from here."

"I'm looking around before I leave, Bianca." He raised an eyebrow, showing he was serious.

She didn't argue with him. In fact, she felt relieved. Once she'd opened the door, she headed to her office. Lamar followed and placed her lunch on her desk. Bianca sat her purse there too and turned her computer back on. She glanced around the room. Everything was the same as she'd left it. She'd probably wait until eating again, considering since she almost got run over.

Lamar asked. "Everything good?"

"Yes," she said. "I don't think they came here."

He backed up towards her doorway. "How much work do you have left? I'd probably call it a half day and go home."

"Not much. Going home early is actually a good idea." Bianca walked closer and stood in front of him in the doorway. "Thank you for walking me back and staying. How much longer with your shift?"

"I should be finished by six tonight," he said.

Should she ask? "Any news about the case?"

Lamar smirked. "No, unless you have additional evidence for me."

Her tongue darted out to lick her lips. The heat between them intensified. "No. Not that I... Unless what happened today was—"

He raised his hand to stop her. "We'll dig further into it. Okay?" Lamar cocked his head to the side. He didn't put his hand down. Instead, he touched her face.

Bianca held back her gasp. "You're not on the clock anymore?"

He whispered. "Technically, I'm on break. Might as well enjoy it. Right?"

Bianca leaned into his touch, keeping firm eye contact with him. "That sounds reasonable enough."

"But I said... I won't do anything until you're ready," he reminded her.

She whispered back, "I'm not stopping you, Lamar."

He smiled for a moment, but then his eyes dropped to her lips. He leaned in.

Bianca closed her eyes, drowning in the intoxicating scent of his woodsy cologne. His free hand cupped her waist, drawing her closer to his hard chest.

Buzz. Buzz. Buzz. Buzz.

Lamar groaned, resting his head against hers. "You can't be serious."

Bianca giggled, but she was annoyed, too.

He backed away and dug into his pocket for his phone. "It's Atkins. We may have a lead on the car."

Bianca flinched.

Chapter 18

Bianca leaned against the doorway of her office. *"We may have a lead on the car."* The scene was in her mind again. *SCREECH!*

"Bianca?" Lamar touched her shoulder. "What's wrong?"

"I was... trying to remember if I recognized the driver." She sighed, opening her eyes. "What did Atkins say?"

"We got an anonymous tip. They spotted the car around Trip's Rentals."

A rented car? To run her over?

Lamar used his thumb to type a message on his phone. "I'm going to head over there now. See whom we can question."

"Do I need to come? I can point something out," she said.

He gestured to her to-go plate on her desk. "You haven't eaten, Bianca. Plus, you've been through enough already. This is not even official. It's a possible lead to nowhere."

"We can ride together. You can drive and I'll eat in the car." She hurried to her desk for her lunch and purse.

"Bianca—" Lamar groaned.

"I'll be fine. I promise to go home after this." She held up her keys in the air. They jingled.

He blew out his cheeks. "All right. Only because you *promise* to go home." He followed her outside to the sidewalk, and Bianca locked her office for the day. She handed Lamar her car keys, and when he unlocked it, he opened the door for her.

He slid into the driver's seat. "Do you ever follow instructions?"

Bianca giggled as she clicked on her seatbelt. She untied the plastic bag holding her to-go plate. "When it's necessary."

He chuckled as he cranked the engine.

"Besides, this gives me an opportunity to tell you my theory," she said.

He backed out of her parking space and onto the main street. "Only if you eat."

Bianca broke the plastic seal on her silverware. Thank goodness her food was still warm. She took a bite and moaned. Nothing compared to home cooking, and like her mother, Judy had amazing culinary skills.

"That good?" Lamar asked.

Bianca swallowed. "Yes. Now, will you hear my theory?"

He stopped in front of a red traffic light. "Go on."

"I may be wrong, but what if the actual killer is onto... me?"

"Whom have you talked to recently?" he asked as the light turned green.

Bianca had her own list of suspects, but nothing was clear. "Camille. I didn't talk to Bruce, but I saw him in the park before I met Susan."

"Susan?"

"Susan Hayward. She's visiting Edenville. She's the woman I was sitting at the table with today." Bianca took another bite from her plate.

"There's nothing to that, Bianca," he said.

She swallowed before answering again. "What about the watch?"

"That doesn't mean we know what led up to him losing it. If he was, in fact, there himself and he met someone there at night, there were probably no witnesses to report a fight or argument."

Bianca took another bite, pondering, as she chewed. Lamar was right. There was nothing to go on. "What about Isaac?"

"Though Isaac admitted to stealing, Luther's not pressing charges. He's back at the car wash," Lamar said. "Unless he's too foolish to take his second chance, I doubt he had anything to do with today."

Bianca agreed, hoping the police got through to the man. Even if he hadn't been driving the car, perhaps he knew who had? Would he know of people trying to implicate Luther? She finished the rest of her meal in a quiet silence with Lamar, and when he pulled into the parking lot of Trip's Rentals, Bianca stuffed her plate and utensil back into the bag, tying it tightly.

There were police cars in the parking lot, along with new cars for travelers and visitors to rent. People rented cars too if theirs needed repairs. They were either locals *or* visitors.

Lamar parked next to another police car and cut the engine. "Let's see what we got, shall we?"

Bianca slid out of the passenger's seat, along with her purse. She carried her empty plate, looking for a nearby trashcan.

"Here you go." Lamar handed Bianca her keys. "I can ride back to the station with Atkins." He gestured to the narrow building with large glass windows.

Bianca followed him inside, only to find Atkins questioning the young man behind the front desk. She spotted a nearby trashcan and slid her bag with her empty plate inside. She also slipped her car keys inside her purse.

"How many Buicks do you have for rent?" Detective Atkins asked the young man.

He typed on his computer. His spiky, dark-blond hair with black ends caught Bianca's eye. "Looks like we have four."

"Were any of them rented recently?" Lamar stepped up to the front desk. He flashed the young man his badge.

The young man cleared his throat. "One."

"What color?" Detective Atkins asked.

Bianca tapped her foot on the tiled floor.

"Royal blue to a..." The young man typed more into the computer. "Barbara Lewis."

Bianca sighed. Was this a wild goose chase? She turned on her heels and returned outside. Scouring the parking lot, Bianca looked for the Buicks. There were many Fords, Chevys, Hondas, and Dodges. Her heels clicked as she walked the concrete.

Pulling her lips in, she wondered if she would find something that didn't belong. Had there been a beige Buick on the lot? Lamar and Atkins could find out. Her eyes shifted upwards. What about security footage? Something on video could shed light on the case.

Then again, what if there was no connection at all? Lamar was right. Perhaps she needed to go home. Rubbing at her shoulder, she pivoted to face the building, only to spot Lamar and Atkins exiting it. Lamar's head shifted from side to side, but when he caught her eye, he sprinted her way.

"What are you doing?" he asked.

She shrugged. "I thought I'd notice something out there." She gestured at the building. "No beige Buicks, I'm guessing?"

Lamar said, "No. At least not at this location."

Bianca's face slackened.

Lamar tilted his head to the side. "Hey, don't worry. We're going to find who's responsible. Even if it's not connected to Luther's case. Okay?"

Bianca's thoughts kept turning, but she agreed. "Okay."

The corners of his mouth turned up. "Now, are you going home, or do I need to follow you to make sure you do?"

She giggled, appreciating his concern. In a way, it cheered her up. "I'm going." She reached for her keys inside her purse. "You don't have to follow me."

"Good. I'll talk to you later." Then he stepped in closer to whisper in her ear. "We'll pick up where we left off next time."

Bianca bit her bottom lip as he backed up and walked away to join Detective Atkins. Swallowing, Bianca sauntered to her car.

Chapter 19

Tuesday had passed with no leads on the driver, who'd almost hit Bianca. Even when she'd told Melanie the story, her sister couldn't believe it. They'd spent most of the evening spinning theories, only to get nowhere. Now it was Wednesday. Bianca went to the office today after working from home the previous day. She wouldn't let anyone stop her from going into town. She wouldn't give in to fear. Lamar had been busy with work too. They weren't able to go out, but he called to check on her. They also shared a few flirtatious banters. Bianca could get used to that.

"Promise me," Melanie said. "If anything happens, you'll call me right away."

Bianca zipped up her purse, grabbing her car keys. "I will. Don't worry."

Casper barked, and she kneeled down to scratch his ears. "I'll see you later."

Satisfied with her petting, he trotted back to his water bowl. Bianca straightened to her feet.

Melanie folded her arms.

"What?"

Her sister's eyebrows squished together. "It doesn't make sense."

"No, it doesn't. Have you talked to Mom this morning?" Bianca hadn't had the guts. Not with her at the hospital. Deborah had been taking her laptop with her to work, but she wasn't leaving Luther's side. When they talked to her the night before, she said he was doing well.

"No. I'll probably call her later," Melanie answered.

Bianca headed to the garage. "I'll see you later."

Her sister nodded, and Bianca walked out the door. The garage door cranked while opening, but she slid into the driver's seat and started the engine. Blowing out her cheeks, she clicked her seatbelt on. Today would be better, but she would keep her eyes open.

Connecting her Bluetooth to her car, she dialed her daughter's number. Might as well check on Alyssa. It was after nine in the morning. She figured she'd be awake by now.

"Mom?" her daughter greeted, though sounding groggy.

"Hey. How's my girl?" Bianca used her side mirrors to back out of her driveway. She hit the remote to close the garage door.

"Okay. I'm still in the bed. What time is it here, anyway?"

Bianca held back a giggle. She'd forgotten about the time difference. "I'm sorry. Did I wake you?"

Her daughter sighed. "Too late now. I'm up."

"I won't keep you long, then. Only wanted to say *hi*. I miss you."

"I miss you too, Mom. How's everyone?" she asked.

Bianca turned out of her neighborhood and onto the main street leading into downtown. "So far, so good." No sense in sharing the details with Alyssa. She was safe where she was. Stopping at a red light, Bianca spotted a familiar car to her left. A beige Buick. The car that almost... Bianca gasped.

"Mom?" Alyssa said. "Are you okay?"

"Yeah. I'm fine. Just saw... someone I know." Close enough. "You get some more sleep and I'll talk to you later. Love you."

"Okay." Alyssa yawned, not asking further questions. "Love you too." She hung up.

Bianca tapped her fingers to the screen on her car, she called Lamar.

"Good morning." His deep voice filled her car.

"Lamar, I think I see the car."

"What?"

"From Monday. The beige Buick. We didn't get a license plate. Did we?"

"No. Why? Where are you?"

"At the corner of Maverick and Main Street, going west." Bianca switched to the far right lane when the light turned green. Thank goodness another car wasn't there. She turned to follow the Buick.

"You're following it. Aren't you?" Lamar asked.

"Yes I am. Whoever this is almost ran me over this week." She took care not to follow too closely, but she tailed the car.

"Can you see who's driving?"

"Not through the dark tinted windows," she said. Where was this person going? Were they alone?

"Bianca. I'm coming. Can you see where it's heading?" he asked.

Stopping in front of another red light, she replied, "I can't tell right now. So far, they're going west on the main road."

"Okay. Stay on the line with me. It could be a different type of car. We can't say for sure it's the same person."

"And what if it is?"

"I'll question them. Don't get out of the car. We don't know whom we're dealing with yet."

"Okay." The car switched lanes and Bianca waited a few seconds before she did the same.

"Anything?" Lamar asked.

"No." Leaving downtown Edenville, the car entered a more remote location. It turned onto a familiar gravel road. "Lamar?"

"What? Talk to me."

"They're heading to the creek," she said.

"It could be anyone, Bianca. Remember that."

She eased on the brake, careful to stay back a little. Bianca turned into the gravel-covered parking spaces by the creek. She chose the spot by a large tree and not just for the shade. Who was driving? Would she recognize them? Or was this as Lamar had said? Someone else driving with no connection to the speeding car.

"What's going on?" Lamar asked. "I'm almost there, Bianca."

Bianca waited for the driver to exit the car. It was not whom she'd expected. It was Camille.

CAMILLE SLID OUT OF the driver's seat and closed the door behind her. Bianca's mouth was agape. *She'd* almost run her over a couple of days ago? Why? Bianca didn't ask many questions at the hotel. What little they'd talked about sparked a desire to get rid of Bianca? Had she been getting too close to the truth?

Bianca's eyebrows scrunched. The car almost hit Bianca and Melanie in their own car before she went to the hotel to meet Camille. And Camille was supposedly *working out* in the hotel gym.

A curvy woman with binoculars caught Bianca's eye for a moment, along with a few older men sitting in camping chairs at the bank with fishing poles in their hands.

"Bianca?" Lamar's voice came through her car speakers.

"It's Camille. Luther's daughter was in the car," she said.

He exhaled. "Oh, boy. Okay. I'm almost there, but remember, it could be a coincidence."

Bianca disconnected her Bluetooth and cut the engine. She put her phone to her ear. "I doubt it. What if she knows something?" Or what if she'd had something to do with Ronald's death?

"Bianca..." he replied. "All I can do is question her. I'm pulling up beside you now."

Bianca hung up the phone as he approached her door. When she opened it, he blocked her from getting out. She turned the ignition and let down her window. "What are you doing?" she asked.

"I'll question her. You stay here. I don't want her to spot you and take off," Lamar said.

Bianca inwardly winced, but she agreed. "All right. I'll do it your way this time."

He narrowed his eyes at her, but he gave a faint smile. Lamar walked over to Camille, who was bent over looking for something.

I bet its Ronald's watch. Bianca let up her window and called her sister. Melanie would want an update.

"At work already?" her sister greeted.

"I think I found the car from Monday."

Melanie choked, and Bianca overheard Casper's barks in the background. "*What?*"

"Yes. Camille was driving," Bianca told her.

"Why would she-That's-What?" Melanie stammered, obviously confused.

"I called Lamar. He's talking to her now." Bianca focused her eyes ahead to read Camille's expressions. So far, the woman folded her arms over her chest. She wasn't smiling, either.

"Can you hear what's going on?" her sister asked.

"No, and he wants me to stay in the car. In case... she's dangerous."

"So... if she killed her husband... Oh, no, Bianca. You need to let the police handle it." There was an audible worry in Melanie's voice. "I don't like this."

"I'll find out what Lamar says. It could be a coincidence. Her car is not uncommon, but... I'm keeping my eyes open," Bianca assured her.

Melanie exhaled. "Okay. You're not telling Mom still, are you?"

"No," Bianca said. Not until they had more evidence. Lamar extended his hand to Camille, and to Bianca's surprise, she took it. Then she slid back into her car and started the engine. Bianca turned her head so she wouldn't see her. The woman left. A few fishermen watched but said nothing. Birds chirped as the wind rustled through the trees. Lamar walked back in her direction. "I have to go. Let me see what Lamar says."

"Call me later," Melanie said and hung up.

Lamar approached her passenger side, and she unlocked the door. He sat inside and shut the door.

"Well?" Bianca asked.

"She said she was at the hotel when the incident happened. She says the hotel can prove her alibi."

Bianca's lips parted. "So... who was driving?"

Lamar pinched the bridge of his nose. "Not sure. The witnesses couldn't give us further information." He turned and faced her. "Like you, I'm stumped."

Bianca leaned back in her driver's seat. "Camille's car, but she wasn't driving. Was it stolen?"

Lamar shook his head. "No reports of a stolen car. Turns out the rental car tip didn't work out either."

Bianca's skin prickled. Not knowing was irritating. Whom was she dealing with? Who was trying to scare her? Or worse… get rid of her?

"I'm heading back to the station," said Lamar.

"Wait." She grabbed his arm. "She acted like she was looking for something."

"What?" Lamar raised an eyebrow.

"The watch we found. Ronald's watch? Did she say why she was here? Did she and her ex meet here prior to his death?" Bianca wondered.

"She claims she hasn't seen him since that night at the restaurant." Lamar paused. "Now that I think about it, she seemed restless. How did she discover this place?"

Bianca tilted her head to the side.

He raised his hands in surrender. "Okay, there may be something here. I'm not spinning theories, but I'll double-check her alibi. For both days."

"Thank you," Bianca said.

"You should go to work. If I have to, I can send a police car to your office," he suggested.

"No, I'll be fine," she reassured him with a soft smile.

He smiled back. He didn't move right away, but after what seemed like an eternity of him taking her in with his eyes, he exited her car.

Bianca cranked her engine and headed for work. She hoped Lamar would find out the truth before someone else got hurt.

BIANCA SHUT DOWN HER computer and checked the clock on her office wall. She'd finished another mockup design for an upcoming beauty salon in town. Now it was time for a break. She'd already had lunch from Richard and Judy's place, and thankfully, no one had attempted to run her over today.

She stretched her arms over her head. Perhaps a walk would help. She wouldn't go far, but a stroll down Main Street would loosen her tight muscles. She grabbed her purse and phone and locked her front door.

The clouds above floated because of the steady breeze, which Bianca was grateful for. Cars drove by and there were people walking on the sidewalks. Bianca clutched her phone in her hand. She and Melanie had checked on her their mother already on a three-way call. Deborah Wallace hadn't sounded like herself in a while, but Bianca wasn't sure what else to do. Adjusting her purse on her shoulder, she walked to the crosswalk.

Looking ahead, she spotted a man walking with his phone in the air. Judging by the scrunch on his face, he wasn't pleased. He moved his phone in another direction. Looking for better reception? He had to be new in Edenville if he wasn't aware where the usual dead zones were.

Bianca crossed the street and inched closer. No harm in helping, but when she recognized his face, she swallowed. Bruce. Though she'd only seen him twice, at the hotel with Camille and at the park, she wouldn't have forgotten his face.

"Need help?" she asked.

"I'm sorry," he replied.

Bianca pointed around her. "This is a poor spot for cell reception." Then she pointed to Ms. Ella's floral shop a few blocks away. "That's a good spot." Might as well go with that story in case she got wind of something interesting. "I was going to stop by and visit her, anyway." Sort of.

Bruce's face slackened. "Thank you." He fell in step beside her. "I appreciate your help."

Bianca replied, "You're welcome. I assume you're visiting Edenville."

He raised an eyebrow.

She continued. "The locals know everyone here, so we notice unfamiliar faces."

He chuckled. "That makes sense. Yes, I'm visiting. Taking care of my sister-in-law. Well... former sister-in-law."

Bianca snapped her fingers. "I think I've seen you. You know Camille Burkes?"

Bruce's jaw clenched. "Yeah, that's her."

"I heard about your brother," she said. "I'm so sorry."

"I'm not." He paused in his tracks, as if he'd just realized his choice of words. "I'm sorry. That sounds... morbid."

Bianca asked, "You weren't close?"

Bruce stuffed his free hand inside his jean pocket. "Not when your parents have you competing all your life." He scanned the concrete for a moment. "I've said too much again." He held up his head. "I'm only here for Camille." He huffed. "I have to give it to Ronald. He picked a good woman. Even if he *didn't* deserve her."

Bianca didn't reply. Only took in the information. Vibrant and yellow and orange roses, which scents varied from fruits and cloves, met her nose. Bianca knew they'd arrived at Ms. Ella's floral shop. "Here we are. You shouldn't have any problems now."

Bruce bobbed his head. "Thanks."

Bianca entered the floral shop but stayed close to the window. Ms. Ella was attending a customer, but she waved from the counter.

Returning the gesture, Bianca perused the floral arrangements by the front window. The glass muffled Bruce's voice, but she could still pick up his conversation.

"Hey, Camille," he said.

Bianca grazed a yellow rose while she listened.

"What?" Bruce said. "What do you mean... a detective asked you some questions? Your car?" He shifted his gaze back and forth, as if to keep his conversation private. "I told you not to worry."

'Don't worry'? What did that mean? About what, specifically?

"Camille, I told you I'd take care of everything," he said.

'Everything'? Something wasn't right.

Bianca admired another bouquet, this time one of tulips. She bought it to seem less suspicious. Camille and Bruce in this together? Why? When Bianca turned to leave after nodding goodbye to Ms. Ella, she found Bruce had gone.

Chapter 20

Thursday morning arrived with no recent case developments. Now at the office, Bianca sent updates about Wallace Designs' grand reopening to her virtual assistant, Veronica, to take care of. Not only did she invite the town, but her first clients too. Hopefully, Chad and Nicole were back in time to celebrate with her. Bianca's mother called before she left for work, and Casper was with the dog sitter. The hospital would discharge Luther by the afternoon and the police were taking him into custody.

Though Bianca did her best to concentrate, she couldn't help her upset stomach. No, clearing Luther's name was not her responsibility. Despite wanting to help her mother, what if her detective skills had run out? Sure, she'd helped in two cases before. That didn't mean she could triumph every time a crime arose in Edenville.

Opening her design for Luther's fundraiser, she adjusted the colors, finally adding his logo along with the address, date, and time. Even though he'd be in jail, she hoped the community was still supporting the cause. The police released the car wash, so it would be open.

Saving the final version of the flier, Bianca emailed the final copy to the email address Luther had given her. Isaac could handle it. She'd done her job, and that was enough. Sitting back in her office chair, Bianca folded her hands in her lap. She wondered if she needed to return to the hospital.

Staring at her clock on the beige wall, she noted it was almost noon. Her mother would need her support, especially if they were taking Luther to jail. Bianca shut down her computer and grabbed her phone and purse. Once she'd locked up, she paced to her Kia Soul.

Sliding into her driver's seat, Bianca started the engine. She blew out her cheeks. She would do her best to be strong for her mother. With little traffic to slow her commute down, Bianca pulled into the hospital parking lot. Despite the visitors' parking being usually full of cars, Bianca found a spot close to the entrance. As soon as she'd cut the engine, a police car pulled up.

She didn't move at first, but when she recognized Lamar and Detective Atkins, she got out and locked her car. Lamar paused in his steps when he saw her. He wore a dark-blue suit this time, but his badge was on his hip, as usual, along with his gun. His jaw clenched and with a nod of his head, he and Atkins went inside.

Bianca followed, and by the time the trio had made it to Luther's room, Bianca's heart broke for her mother, who stood next to Luther. Luther's gaze averted from the police for a second, but then he faced them.

"Can I at least have a moment?" he asked, gesturing at Bianca's mother. "I agree to come quietly."

Lamar nodded his head, stepping to the side. Atkins, however, was ready to make the arrest.

Bianca touched a hand to her chest. She watched her mother embrace Luther, wrapping her arms around his neck. She couldn't understand their whispers to each other, and frankly, Bianca didn't want to. When Luther pulled back, he planted a soft kiss on her mother's lips. He cupped her cheek for a second, but then stepped forward, turning his back to Detective Atkins.

He read him his rights. "You have the right to remain silent. Anything you say can and will be used against you in a court of law..." His voice thinned out as he led Luther to the entrance. Nurses and patients didn't hesitate to stare, but Bianca sprinted to her mother's side.

When her mother noticed she was there, she opened her arms for an embrace. "Bianca..." Her voiced choked as tears spilled down her face.

Lamar cleared his throat. "I'd see about getting him a good lawyer."

Her mother pulled back from her daughter's embrace. Her expression was blank. "If you would... excuse me, please." Deborah walked down the hall to the restrooms.

Bianca stared after her.

"I don't like this either," Lamar said.

"You're just... doing your job."

Lamar opened his mouth to answer, but his walkie-talkie sounded off.

"Sims, we've got a situation outside." Atkins's voice said. "We've got the suspect's daughter here. She's hysterical."

Lamar groaned and ran down the hallway.

Bianca's eyes widened.

"What's going on?" her mother asked, emerging from the ladies' room.

Bianca followed Lamar through the automatic doors, only to spot Camille trying to talk to her father inside the police car. Lamar stepped between Camille and Atkins.

"We need you to calm down, Ms. Burkes," he said to her.

"But he's got nothing to do with it!" Camille yelled as tears poured down her face. "He didn't kill anyone. He couldn't have!"

Deborah Wallace arrived, and stood next to Bianca as they witnessed what looked like a scene from a movie. Her mother told her Camille had visited her father in the hospital, but she noticed nothing strange in her behavior then.

"If you want to come down to the station, you can," Detective Atkins added.

Camille cried. "Dad, I'm sorry! I'm so sorry."

"Camille," Luther said, although his tone had a warning attached to it.

Camille raked her fingers through her hair. "He was only trying to protect me..."

Bianca gasped. Her mother gripped her arm in obvious anticipation. A few spectators watched as they passed by, but they entered the hospital.

"Ms. Burkes, I'm going to ask you to step aside?" Lamar asked.

"Camille, stop talking!" Luther's raspy voice shouted at her.

She wrung her hands together. "There's more to the story..." Her voice trembled. Then she covered her mouth as her shoulders shook. The tears took over.

"Bianca..." her mother whispered.

"I know," she replied.

BIANCA AND HER MOTHER sat in plastic chairs in the police station waiting area. Camille showing up at the hospital had changed everything. As soon as she'd said, "There's more to the story," Lamar and Detective Atkins had urged her to come to the police station. What did she realize that Luther didn't want her to tell the police?

Though Bianca hated to consider both father and daughter had handled Ronald's death, the notion was a possibility. Doors buzzing and phones ringing filled Bianca's ears. Her mother adjusted in her seat next to Bianca by the water fountain, watching the police officers doing administration work and answering phones.

"I knew there was an explanation," her mother said.

Bianca looked up at her mother. "What do you mean by that?"

Her mother added. "If Camille had something to do with the killing, and this is his way of protecting her. He's making a mistake."

"He took the fall for her?" Bianca had suspected, but she'd never fully believed it.

"We'll find out today," her mother replied. "But if she's hiding something, I hope she's telling everything to the police now." Her mother patted her purse. "If not, I'm here to bail Luther out."

Bianca's mind replayed scenarios. Camille killing Ronald? If so, why had Luther been knocked out... unless he'd faked it? If he and Ronald had had an altercation that explained the bump, but what if he'd resumed consciousness sooner, before Bianca had arrived?

Lamar and Detective Atkins emerged from the hallway. They shared a few words in a quiet tone, but then Lamar walked over to Bianca and her mother.

Deborah Wallace stood to her feet. "Well? Did she confess everything?"

Bianca reached up to grab her mother's hand.

Lamar exhaled, folding his arms over his chest. "She says she was at the car wash. She came to talk with her dad and Ronald followed her. Luther overheard them arguing and took his own gun with him outside. Ronald had grabbed her but let go because of Luther's threat to shoot. He had Camille leave and told her to keep quiet, trying to protect her. She was also our anonymous caller that night too.

He struggled with Ronald and the gun went off, but he says Ronald didn't appear hit. That's when Ronald knocked him out. Camille didn't do anything except to report everything she witnessed to the police. Luther was the only one holding the gun. No one else witnessed what happened, so it looks like he still did it all. "

"That *doesn't* mean he killed Ronald," Bianca's mother said. "If he was protecting himself and Camille, especially if Ronald grabbed her and..."

Lamar's face softened. "We're going to sort this out. Until then, Luther's in a holding cell. I have a few more questions to ask Camille, so it's not over."

"Can I talk to him?" her mother asked, her hands clutched together.

Lamar motioned to Detective Sims. "Give Mrs. Wallace a few minutes with Mr. Burkes."

As soon as her mother had disappeared down the hallway, Bianca faced Lamar. "Thank you. She's ready to post bail if need be. No matter the cost."

Lamar rubbed the back of his head. "I figured."

"Where is she?" A man burst through the front doors with a loud shout.

Both Lamar and Bianca whirled around to identify who was shouting. Bruce Cartwright?

A few officers ran to the scene. Bruce's brow beaded with sweat. "Tell me where she is right now!" he yelled.

Lamar dashed ahead with a few more officers, holding Bruce back. "Sir, I need you to calm down and tell me what's going on. Who are you looking for?"

"Where's Camille?" Bruce said through gritted teeth as two officers held him back by the shoulders.

"She's in for questioning, that's all," Lamar assured him.

Bianca stood, frozen. The pictures of Camille and Bruce on social media flashed through her mind. There was no doubt he cared about her. Did he suspect something, too? Was this case all a tangled mess?

"Where *is* she?" Bruce shouted as the officers pinned him to a plastic chair. It scraped the floors as he struggled with them. "Camille! Camille!"

"I need you to calm down first!" Lamar raised his voice. "Making a scene won't help her."

Bruce huffed, finally relaxing his arms. "All right. All right." The officers holding him let him go.

"Now," Lamar said, "do you know anything else we should?"

Bruce shook his head. Then he rested it in his large hands.

Lamar spoke to the officers around him still. "Watch him."

Bianca took out her phone.

Lamar returned to her side. "It's best you and your mother leave. No telling who else will pop in today."

"You need to see this," she said, holding up her phone to him.

He focused on the screen. "Okay. Instagram page of... Camille." His eyes shot back to Bruce, who didn't move still.

"This was posted a few days ago. If something's going on between them, don't you think it's worth looking into?" She tilted her head.

He sighed. "What are you getting at, Bianca?"

"I'm not sure, but Camille said she wanted to hear Ronald out. Like... she wanted to give him another chance. They were at the restaurant together." She pointed to the posted photo. "Why so close with his brother, then? This picture is recent."

Lamar looked upward. "I'll keep it in mind. Make sure your mother is okay. Go back to work."

At least he hadn't shut her down completely. "Thank you for hearing me out."

He gave her a faint smile. "I'm learning to."

BIANCA WALKED SIDE by side with her mother, exiting the police station. Her mother's arm looped through hers and judging by her damp eyes, Deborah had shed a few more tears after visiting Luther in the holding cell. Bianca stopped in her tracks, unlooping her arm, and pulled out a handkerchief from her purse.

She handed it to her mother, touching her shoulder. "I'm sorry, Mom. I can't... imagine what you're feeling."

Her mother sniffled. "Luther thought he was making the right decision. I can understand a parent protecting their child." Motioning to her daughter's car, parked alongside her own, Bianca understood the gesture that her mother needed time to decompress. Her car beeped when Bianca disarmed her alarm, and once inside, she locked the doors after them. They'd talked a bit more. She'd offered her mother a ride, seeing how upset she was at the hospital, but Deborah Wallace insisted on driving herself.

"Someone... who... none of this makes sense to me," her mother said.

"Did Camille notice anyone else when she was at the car wash? Or when she left it?"

Her mother shook her head. "Luther cannot figure out the missing piece so the police are only working with the evidence. It's possible Camille's full story can help him, but not by much."

Bianca's lips parted.

"What?" Her mother's eyebrow raised.

"Isaac. Luther's manager. What if *he* knocked Luther out?"

"I don't understand why he would," her mother replied. "Luther has done nothing but give Isaac chance after chance. Luther took him under his wing when Isaac couldn't get a job. Wanting to help him get his life on track."

"Has Isaac ever been to prison?" Bianca asked. She was sure Lamar knew as much.

"Attempted robbery, from what Luther told me. Isaac was in his early twenties when it happened, but had been part of the wrong crowd since he was a teenager. His mother's dead."

"So why steal from Luther after all he's done for him?"

Her mother's face softened. "Some people, after being disappointed, feel they can't trust anyone. No matter if the person is kind to them."

Bianca tapped her fingers on her pants leg. Perhaps Isaac would talk to her if she could convince him. Finalizing everything for the car wash would be a good reason. She faced her mother. "Mom, why don't you go home? Do you have any work to do? Get your mind off things."

Her mother's eyebrows furrowed. "Yes, but my assistant, Breann, knows I'm—"

"I need to finish one thing before I head back to my office." Bianca focused her eyes on her. "Trust me. We're going to prove Luther's innocence."

Her mother opened her lips to reply but only nodded her head. With one last hug, her mother returned to her car. Bianca grabbed her phone after watching her mother leave the parking lot.

Isaac answered. "Ms. Wallace?"

"Hi, Isaac," she said. "Is this a bad time?"

"No." He gave no more information. Was he feeling remorseful since Luther didn't press charges? He should have after giving Isaac a second chance, knowing his record.

"Great. I wanted to make sure the fliers were good."

"Everything's on schedule now that we're reopening. The fliers are going up. I... haven't filled in Mr. Burkes yet, but I will."

Bianca tapped her fingers on the steering wheel. "Isaac, I need to ask you something. It's important."

"Go for it," he said. He kept his tone even, as if holding back any emotion.

"Can you tell me why you were stealing from Mr. Burkes?" she asked.

"I was borrowing the money. I was going to give it back," he said.

"Why, Isaac? Mr. Burkes has done nothing but give you a job, entrusted you as a manager. Why would—"

"So what?!" he yelled at her. After a moment, cleared his throat. "Sorry."

"It's okay," she said, willing her pulse to slow down. "It just doesn't make sense to me, Isaac. I thought Mr. Burkes was like a father to you. Why betray him like this?"

Isaac didn't respond, and she wondered if her statement had gotten to him. She pushed further.

"I get it," Bianca said. "It's stupid of him, right? Why should he care about you? He knew your past. Everyone else didn't give you a chance, so why should he believe in someone like you?"

Isaac didn't reply.

Bianca continued. "It's called grace, Isaac. Compassion. Mr. Burkes obviously sees potential in you. He wants you to live up to it before it's too late. How old are you again?"

He exhaled. "Thirty... seven."

Bianca bobbed her head. "It's time, Isaac. We all have to grow up eventually and face situations like mature adults. Do you want to live like this in five years? Ten?"

No response.

"You can start today. Choose to live a better life now," she said, praying her words mattered to him. "Mr. Burkes believes in you, and... I do, too."

"I... I can actually believe he didn't press charges," he said. His voice sounded less defensive.

"Take the chance, Isaac," Bianca said. "I'll see you at the car wash."

Isaac didn't reply, so she hung up.

Bianca rested against the headrest of her car. *Tap. Tap.* She jerked in her seat, only to find Lamar at her window.

Bianca reached for her keys in her purse, started the engine, and let down the window.

"Well?" Lamar asked. "Any new information I can use?"

She chuckled. "I could've been on the phone with a client. Which I was. Finalizing the plans for the car wash."

Lamar leaned against the car. "I caught some of what you said to him. You gave some good advice."

She smiled, detecting his woodsy cologne since he stood close. Her skin prickled. "Thank you."

He motioned to the street. "Now, will you go back to work?" His smile gave him away, despite the seriousness of his tone.

Her lips curved into a grin. "As you wish."

Chapter 21

Bianca parked her car outside of her office and cut the engine. This had been another long day. Luther's arrest. Camille's full confession. At least she could close out Thursday after getting in some work, but she hoped she'd gotten through to Isaac. Slipping out of the driver's seat and locking the car, she stepped onto the curb. Her office keys jingled as she grabbed them from her purse, but when she gazed at the cracked door, she gasped.

Bianca was sure she'd locked the door. Was she being robbed? She looked through the window. The sitting area looked the same. What about her computer? Had someone stolen that? Grabbing her phone, she called Lamar.

"Bianca, I can't—"

"Someone broke into my office," she said. She heard rustling in the background.

"When? Where are you in the building?"

"I'm outside. I haven't gone in," she said.

"Wait until I get there," he ordered. "Stay on the line with me, okay?"

"Okay."

He asked, "What do you see?"

"The door's cracked, but I locked it before I left for the hospital earlier." Her eyes shifted around her. Was someone behind the building? What could they want to steal from her?

"What else?" he asked.

Bianca heard the crank of an engine. "I don't..."

"Okay. Atkins and I are on our way. Get back into your car. We'll be there soon."

She didn't hesitate to do what he'd asked, and when she'd locked herself back in her car, she breathed easier. Had anyone seen anything? Bianca's office wasn't too far from Ms. Ella's floral shop. Had she noticed any suspicious activity? She had to have seen it. If she wanted to, she could report the news in town.

"Bianca, are you all right?" Lamar asked.

The tightness in her chest eased. He was coming. She wouldn't have to face an intruder alone, although her skin pricked with irritation. Thieves had nothing better to do? If they needed help, why not ask for it? Why take from innocent people?

Perhaps something was wrong with her front door. Did the lock need to be fixed? Bianca shook her head. That couldn't be. She'd never had a problem locking up the office before.

A police car pulled up next to her, and she gave a faint smile when Lamar hopped out of the car. Detective Atkins followed once he'd cut the engine. Both officers took out their guns, and Lamar mouthed to her, "Stay there."

She nodded and placed her phone in her lap. Bianca wondered about calling her mother, but thought better of it at the moment. She would tell her later. Bianca wanted to be certain of the situation first before calling family and friends.

Bianca wrung her hands together, praying nothing was missing. Not with her grand reopening approaching. She had a business to run, and this wasn't a hiccup she'd planned for. A groan escaped her mouth just as Lamar emerged from the front door. He motioned for her to come out and Bianca did, grabbing her phone and locking her car.

Lamar's gun was back on his hip. "Atkins is checking a second time, but we saw nothing."

Bianca's lips parted. "But the door was open."

"Are you sure you locked it?" he asked.

She eyeballed him. "Why wouldn't I? With the rate of crime increasing in this town?"

He rubbed at his temples. "Sorry, I have to ask."

She sighed. "Was anything missing?"

He returned his hands to his sides. "Not that I can tell." He gestured for her to follow him. "See if you notice anything, in case we missed something."

Bianca's eyes roamed the sitting area. The chairs were still in place. The coffee table hadn't shifted from its spot. So far, so good.

Lamar followed her as she sprinted to her office. She placed a hand on her chest to find her computer in its place. Her office chair hadn't moved.

Detective Atkins walked out of her adjoined restroom. "Nothing. I'll check around the back."

"Thank you," Bianca replied to him. She folded her arms over her chest once she and Lamar were alone. "I don't get it. Someone breaks in but takes nothing."

"Yeah, it seems odd." His eyes roamed around her office. "Nothing looks out of place?"

"No. Everything's here. Unless..."

"What?" he asked.

"This was only to... scare me," she whispered.

"Bianca, why would someone—"

"I keep coming back to Ronald's killing. What if I'm being followed? What if someone else was there?"

Lamar made a steeple with his hands, exhaling deeply. Then his hands returned to his side. "Bianca, all I can tell you is someone tampered with your lock. Obviously, whatever they were looking for, they didn't find it here. If you're being followed, I can send another officer out here to follow you home when you leave for the day. Do you want to file a report with the information you told us?"

She replied, "Yes."

"Okay," he said. Then he reached out and touched her shoulder. "Are you okay?"

She covered his hand with hers. "I'm okay. Thanks for coming so quickly. I appreciate it."

His eyes softened. "You're welcome." Then he dropped his hand back to his side.

Atkins walked back inside. "Nothing back there. What are you thinking?" he asked Lamar.

"We'll file a report based on what she told us. There's nothing left to do. Hopefully, they don't come back to finish the job." Lamar faced Bianca. "Do you have an alarm system?"

"I'm looking into one."

"Good." He faced Atkins. "I'll meet you back in the car."

Atkins nodded at her and left the room again.

"Call me if anything else happens, or if you think anything looks suspicious," Lamar said.

"I will," Bianca answered.

"And... I'll keep in mind what you said. You are a witness to a murder case, so we'll keep our eyes open. All right?"

She nodded. "Okay. Thanks for... not completely dismissing my... hunches."

The corner of his mouth curved. "I'm getting used to your hunches. Have a nice day at work. I'll talk to you later." He winked at her and left.

Bianca followed him, glancing at her sign on her front door reading *closed*. It was a better idea to finish her workload at home. She didn't have any new clients today.

Chapter 22

Casper barked, and his tail wagged when Bianca walked through the door after closing the garage door. Melanie looked at the watch on her wrist.

"You're home already?" she asked.

Bianca motioned to the couch, and Melanie followed her. Casper trotted to his water bowl. Melanie had picked him up from the dog sitter. While she could watch him most days since she frequently worked from home, but on busier days, Melanie didn't have time to walk him.

"I talked to Mom. Luther's daughter showed up?" Melanie asked.

Bianca nodded. "Something... else happened today."

"What?"

"Someone... broke into my office while I was at the police station with Mom," Bianca said.

Melanie's body jerked. "What? No! Are you okay?" She reached out and touched her shoulders. "Are you hurt? Who—"

Bianca placed her hands on tops of Melanie's. "I'm fine. Nothing stolen, and I called Lamar right away."

Melanie dropped her hands. "Who would do such a thing?"

Bianca pulled in her lips for a moment. "I'm not sure, but I feel it's related to this murder case."

Melanie touched her own throat.

"Mel, there's no telling if we're dealing with one person or more. What if the killer has an accomplice? I suspect they did it to scare me. Lamar and Detective Atkins didn't find fingerprints, but the door was open and I'm certain I locked it."

Melanie said, "I'm still confused why? Were you getting close to something? Did you find out anything else?"

Bianca had already filled in Melanie on the rest of today's events. "Mom and I were at the hospital. Then Camille showed up saying she was at the car wash. Bruce showed up later at the station. Not to mention Isaac stealing from Luther."

Melanie sighed. "I wonder..."

"What?" Bianca asked.

Melanie continued, "I just talked to mom. Luther's bail is at $100,000. They're saying voluntary manslaughter. According to Luther, Ronald hit him, taking his gun. Mom's working on getting at least ten percent to get him out of jail with the help of a bondsman."

"Something's out of place." Then Bianca sat up. "Camille said she was there at the car wash. She visited her dad. They're patching things up. What if Ronald followed her?"

Melanie tilted her head. "Okay. I can picture that since you said he had a temper, and they threw him out of the restaurant."

Bianca added. "Let's say she's getting ready to leave and Ronald catches her in the parking area. Luther comes outside because of the yelling. I wouldn't blame him for having a gun on him to protect himself as a businessman. He and Ronald get into a fight. The gun goes off."

Melanie raked her fingers through her hair. "But you found Ronald on his stomach *inside* the wash bay and there was no sign of Camille. Luther was unconscious."

Bianca snapped her fingers. "That's what I can't figure out. If Luther faked passing out, they could have moved his body." Why would *the actual fight* happen in the parking lot instead of inside the wash bay, anyway? She couldn't forget her theory about the creek, either.

"But who?" her sister asked.

A *tsk* escaped Bianca's mouth. "I hate to suspect Isaac. He seems like a good guy who grew up in the wrong environment."

"Why would *he* kill Ronald?" Melanie wondered. "They didn't know each other."

Bianca gasped. "That'd be *weird* if they did." Suppose Isaac jumped into the fight to defend Luther, who's like a dad to him? He spotted trouble and wanted to help, even if he didn't like Luther that much."

Or was Isaac framing Luther? What if he had second thoughts, considering he already had a record, and panicked, willing to frame Luther at that point rather than take the rap himself?

"I can't imagine Isaac doing something like that to Luther, anyway. If anything, he could've been defending Luther. That's if he was there." Melanie paused, exhaling a deep breath. "Who... hates Luther this much? Is this revenge?"

"I can't say," Bianca whispered.

Melanie added. "Me, neither, but Isaac is... like a son to Luther."

"Based on his attitude today, I wasn't sure if he cared about the man. I hope I got through to him when we talked today. Who knows how that will turn out," Bianca replied. Her eyebrows furrowed as she stared at her blank computer screen.

"What? Bianca?" Melanie waved her hand in front of her. Casper's collar jingled as he walked past them down the hallway.

"Mel..." Her eyes widened. "I have a thought... but it's out there."

"How 'out there'?"

Bianca motioned with her arm. "Like way, way far out there."

Melanie's lips perked up, but she didn't laugh. "Okay. What is it?"

"What if...? No, that's not possible." *Buzz. Buzz.* Bianca grabbed her purse for her phone. When she noticed Alyssa FaceTiming her, her heart warmed. Accepting the call, Melanie leaned in closer to say *hi* to her niece.

Alyssa's curls were in a high ponytail, but her skin glowed. "Hi, Mom. Hi, Aunt Mel!"

Melanie took the phone from her sister. "So... how's California? Have you visited any places lately?" Rising to her feet, she walked toward the window with Bianca's phone.

Bianca's mouth hung agape. "Hello? She called *me*?"

Melanie waved her comment away, enjoying being the cool aunt she always claimed to be.

Bianca rushed to her feet, walking to stand behind Melanie.

"Well... like I told Mom, it's a lot bigger than Edenville," Alyssa replied. "Dad's taking me out to dinner tonight. 'Father-daughter' dinner, he said."

"That's thoughtful of him," Bianca said. She had to give it to her ex-husband for trying to rebuild his relationship with their only child together.

"How's Kendrick?" Melanie asked. Casper trotted back into the living room with another chew toy in his mouth.

"We're okay so far. He's on vacation with his family. They're taking a road trip to Arizona, he told me." Alyssa's eyes shifted between them both. "Anything interesting going on in town?"

Bianca bit her bottom lip. No way had Alyssa heard about Edenville's news in California. If Luther went to prison, she'd found out when she returned home. "Well... Luther's..."

"He's...?" Alyssa raised her eyebrows.

"He's in jail," Melanie blurted out.

"Mel?" Bianca face-palmed. Not quite the way she'd wanted to tell her daughter.

Alyssa blinked. "*What*?"

"We know he's innocent, but he's being framed for murder," Bianca explained.

Alyssa sat back in her chair. "No wonder Grandma sounded down last night. I asked her if she was okay, but she wouldn't tell me anything."

"Perhaps she didn't want to worry you," Melanie said.

Bianca grabbed her phone from her sister. "Alyssa, everything's okay."

"You really believe he's innocent, Mom?" Alyssa asked.

"The truth will come out, eventually."

"Let's hope so. I can tell Grandma cares about him, and I'd hate for her to get hurt." Alyssa rubbed her head.

Bianca touched her sensitive stomach with her free hand. Alyssa wasn't getting triggered, was she? Had this brought up terrible memories for her? "Sweetie, are you—?"

Alyssa smiled. "I'm okay, Mom. The online counseling sessions are helping. So far, I've gone to two and I like it."

"That's good," Melanie said. "And... we met Luther's daughter. Apparently, they're reconnecting. It's good for Luther, but bad timing."

Alyssa's forehead wrinkled. "His daughter's there?"

"Yeah, remember he told us he had a daughter and a granddaughter?" Bianca reminded her.

Alyssa nodded. "I guess I'm surprised after what he told us before. That they weren't close."

Bianca recalled that too, at one of their family dinners. Luther's slackened face had shown he'd wished things had been different with his family.

"Anyway, I gotta go. I hope the police will clear his name soon. I can't imagine him doing this. Love you both." Alyssa waved goodbye before ending the call.

"Bye, honey." Bianca waved back.

Melanie blew her niece a kiss.

Like a son kept replaying in Bianca's mind. How Luther hadn't pressed charges against Isaac, though he'd stole from him. Giving him a job as manager after his past with the law. Why? Who was to say Isaac wouldn't return to that lifestyle? It was nice to have faith in the man, but maybe Isaac needed to face the consequences of his actions. Bianca sighed. If Alyssa ever got into trouble, she wouldn't give up on her daughter.

Bianca gasped.

Melanie touched her arm. "What's wrong?" she asked, her forehead etched in apparent worry.

Bianca would have never considered it before, but the way her skin prickled wouldn't let her shake the notion. Was it possible that Isaac was...?

"Bianca?" Melanie shook her arm. "Talk to me."

She swallowed. "I still have a thought."

"What?"

"It's possible that... what if... Isaac is... Luther's son?"

Melanie's mouth cracked open. "No way."

"He was married before to Camille's mother. Luther had a past before he came to Edenville. What if Isaac was from another marriage? A previous relationship?" Bianca wondered.

"What... he... I think Mom would know. She knows about his daughter. She would have known if Luther had a son. I think the whole town would unless—"

"He didn't *want* anyone to know." Bianca finished her sentence. "Something doesn't feel right about this. You're right about one thing, though."

"What?" Melanie asked.

"Mom knowing." Bianca hadn't been planning on visiting her mother that evening—though she never needed a reason to go home—but she couldn't defer an impromptu visit.

"What if Luther's been bad news from the beginning? I get it. Mom wants to see the best in him. She's been alone a long time. What if this is some twisted plot? Even if Mom's not aware, she deserves the truth."

Bianca tapped her phone on her cheek. "She does, and we'll hear her out. The last thing I want her to assume is we're attacking her and Luther's relationship."

Her sister picked up Casper, who pawed at her feet. "I guess... it's Mom's house for dinner?"

"Right," Bianca replied.

Chapter 23

Jasper's and Horas', Deborah Wallace's golden and dark-brown Yorkies', barks could be detected outside the front of her mother's Cape Cod home. Melanie pulled out her spare key while Bianca held Casper.

"I wonder if we should have called," Melanie said. "She's probably resting with everything going on."

"Let's see." Bianca adjusted her dog in her arms, and when they opened the door, Horas' and Jasper's barks pierced through their ears. "Mom." Bianca placed Casper on the floor as Melanie closed the door behind them.

"Maybe she's in the kitchen," Melanie said.

Horas jumped on his hind legs, but it didn't appear as if he wanted to play. Jasper ran ahead of them, followed by Casper and Horas, leading the women to the kitchen.

"Mom, where are you—" Melanie froze in place.

Bianca's body stiffened when she saw a hand on the floor behind the kitchen island. Had their mother passed out? Rushing to her side, Bianca turned her mother to face the ceiling as opposed to the tiled floor. Melanie pulled out her phone and called 911. Bianca held her mother's hand, checking for any bumps or bruises on her head. Had the back door been broken into?

"Is she breathing?" Melanie asked, despite her shaky voice.

Bianca leaned over and checked and noticed her mother's chest rising and falling. Her Yorkies whimpered while Casper licked her fingers. "Get a wet towel."

Melanie managed, putting her phone down using the speaker. Then she joined Bianca on the floor, on her knees. "An ambulance is on its way. The police too."

Bianca grabbed her phone from her pocket and sent a text to Lamar.

Emergency at my mom's. Come quick!

Then she dabbed her mother's forehead with the towel after stuffing her phone back into her pocket. "Mom, can you hear us?"

"Mom?" Melanie cried out.

Both Jasper and Horas barked again, and to Bianca's surprise, her mother moaned. She could hear them? Would she remember what had happened?

"Mom?" Bianca repeated.

Her mother's eyes fluttered open. Her lips parted to speak. "Bi... Bianca?"

"I'm here. We're both here," she said.

Melanie touched a hand to her chest. "Thank God."

Her mother moved as if to sit up, and her daughters helped.

"Careful," Melanie said. "You should get checked out if you have a head injury. The police and an ambulance are on their way."

Her mother shook her head. "But I..." She touched her forehead. "They didn't knock me out."

Bianca asked. "What?"

"I came in here to start dinner and someone grabbed me from behind and put some type of towel over my nose and mouth," her mother explained.

"Oh, no," Melanie said.

"Mom, when the police arrive, tell them that," Bianca said.

Her mother shook her head. "I don't understand. Who would do such a thing?"

Bianca's body tensed. She hoped the police would find who'd attacked her mother. She was tired of her family being threatened. Hearing sirens outside, Melanie rose to her feet to answer the door. She'd already put her mother dogs in one of the spare bedrooms. Bianca knew as soon as the police arrived, they would flood her with questions. "Mom, I have to ask you something, and I need you to tell me."

"What is it?" Her mother rubbed the back of her neck.

"Does Luther have a son?" she asked plainly. No sense in beating around the bush.

Her mother's eyes widened, and her breath caught in her throat.

Bianca overheard the voices approaching, hearing Melanie direct them inside over the sound of the dogs barking. "Mom, trust me. This is important."

Her mother squeezed her eyes shut. "Yes."

Bianca's breathing slowed. Now the ultimate question. "Is it Isaac Murphy?"

Her mother nodded her head. Her eyes still closed.

Bianca's mouth fell open. Suspicion confirmed.

MELANIE WHISPERED, "She said *yes*?"

Bianca folded her arms as the medics checked her mother's vitals. Lamar and the other officers were looking for any signs of a break-in. He stood by the kitchen table with his notepad as he took notes of her mother's story. Melanie and Bianca weren't to go anywhere. They were next.

Bianca nodded in response to her sister. "And she confirmed it was Isaac."

Melanie covered her mouth with one hand. "I... can't believe it."

"Me, neither."

"Why didn't she tell us before?"

"It wasn't her story to tell, but this case changes everything," Bianca said.

"Ladies," Lamar said as he approached them.

"Detective," Melanie replied.

Bianca gave a faint smile, not knowing how to process her mother's news.

"What time did you arrive?" Lamar asked.

"About 6:15," Melanie said.

"You have a key?" he continued.

"We both have spare keys in case there's an emergency," Bianca explained.

He motioned with his hand. "Go on."

"I unlocked the door," Melanie added. "Our mother's dogs were barking and when we walked inside, one of them led us to her. She was on the floor."

Bianca chimed in. "I checked to see if she was still breathing. Melanie called the police. She said that someone had attacked her and put a towel over her face. She passed out on the floor."

"Was this a burglary, detective?" Melanie asked.

"From what we've seen, nothing's missing," Lamar said. "Atkins will confirm when he finishes checking the perimeter." "Would anyone want to hurt your mother? Possibly steal from her?"

"No," Melanie said. "Everyone we know in Edenville knows and loves our mom."

"Not everyone in Edenville now is a native," Bianca added. "What about Isaac Murphy? Bruce Cartwright?"

Lamar raised his hands as if to stop her. "Hold on, Bianca, before you go accusing people, let's deal with the facts, please. Did you see anyone leave the house when you arrived? A car speed away? Someone run away on foot?"

Bianca exhaled a deep breath. "No. I didn't think to check since *my mother* was on the floor." She didn't mean for her tone to sound rude, but what had he expected?

His face softened. "I'm sorry."

Melanie said, "Can I check on my mother now?"

Lamar stepped to the side. Melanie walked past him and the dogs, who were lapping at their water bowls. The police allowed them out of the room. Casper amused himself by playing with a fallen leaf from one of her mother's potted plants in the living room. Bianca stepped forward to follow her sister, but she stopped.

"Who could have done this?" she asked.

"We'll find out," Lamar said.

"Do you... know where Luther is?"

"He made bail, so I suspect he'll be here once he realizes your mother's condition," he replied.

Bianca recalled Melanie saying their mother was working to get his ten percent to make bail. If he'd had anything to do with her mother's attack, he owed her mother back every penny and then some.

"Bianca?" Lamar inched closer, but he didn't touch her.

She shrugged. "If I remember something, I'll tell you."

His face turned serious. "Trust me. We'll find who did this. If there's any connection to Luther's case, we'll determine that, too. I'm not watching blindly from the sidelines here, Bianca."

"You'll do your job, as always." She sighed, releasing some of the tension in her muscles.

"One of you should stay with your mother tonight," he suggested. "She's refusing to go to the hospital, claiming she's fine."

Bianca bobbed her head. Her mother could be stubborn. Bianca was sure the trip to the hospital was to ensure her mother suffered no further injuries, but no sense in trying to convince Deborah Wallace when she decided something.

"I'll even assign an officer to stay and keep watch overnight," he added.

"Thank you. I'm sure my mother will appreciate that." Needing a moment to herself, Bianca headed for the front door. "I need some air." As she opened the door, she met Luther Burkes in the doorway with a raised fist, ready to knock. Bianca's stomach burned. She didn't let him inside, standing as a barrier between him and her mother.

"Bianca, what's going on? I made bail. Where's your mother? I've been calling her, and she didn't answer, so I came over. What are the police doing here?" His face etched with worry.

Bianca wouldn't yell. "Someone attacked her."

His body jerked. "Then I should see—"

Bianca pressed a hand to his hard chest. "Luther, I respect you. I believe you care about my mother, but this is going too far. What do you *need* to tell me? They may connect this to the charges against you. It's too coincidental otherwise. The police will find out eventually if you don't tell them everything. What are you hiding? You're putting my mother and my family in danger and I *won't* have it!"

Luther raised his hand in a gesture of surrender. Then he ran it over his stubble face while the other hand rested to his side. He walked into her mother's yard. Bianca followed.

His bottom lip quivered. "I'm sorry, Bianca. I love your mother. If I'm honest, this is the first time I've been in love. At my age." He released a chuckle, but continued. "I tried to be a good man but made mistakes. I faced the consequences, but unfortunately, many people were hurt."

"You mean your son? Isaac?" Bianca asked, folding her arms over her chest.

Luther gasped, but then he nodded his head. "How did you...?"

"I suspected, but then my mom... She confirmed it. Don't blame her for telling me."

He sniffled. "I won't. Isaac's mother and I split soon after we were married. I found out about him when he was ten. I took him in, but I wasn't the father he needed. Then I married Camille's mother not too long after that, but blending our families didn't work. Isaac was a troubled teen, but I kept reaching out to him. He left home. Got into trouble with gangs. When Camille's mother and I split, I started a new life here, but my daughter blamed me for our divorce, saying I 'broke up the family.' I guess I did."

"Why didn't you tell us about Isaac?" Bianca wondered.

"I meant to, but being divorced twice... failing at both my marriages... being estranged from both my children. I..." He didn't finish.

Bianca rubbed at her arm. "And Isaac's mother?"

He said, "Her car went off the road years ago. She took to drinking. They didn't find the body."

"I'm so sorry."

"Your mother knows. I told her to keep it quiet because I wanted your family to get to know me first. I thought my past would be too much. Not to mention Isaac having... a record."

"By hiding your past? How's that *letting us get to know you*?" she asked.

"I apologize. Bianca, I want to make things better. I can't lose the rest of my family," he said. "Or... you all. You're the family I always wanted."

"Before someone else gets hurt, we need to figure out who's doing this," Bianca replied.

Chapter 24

Once Luther had entered her mother's house, he dashed to Deborah's side. At the breakfast table, she sat with the EMTs. Melanie eyeballed Luther, but she stepped to the side, allowing him to embrace their mother. Bianca shot glances at Luther too. Lamar and Atkins were talking, while a few officers took photos in her mother's kitchen.

Melanie hurried over to her sister. "What's he doing here?"

"He came to see Mom," Bianca replied.

"Hasn't he done enough?"

Bianca took her hand and led her to the hallway. "You're upset."

Melanie's eyes bugged. "Someone *attacked* our mother, Bianca. Looks like I'm more upset than you."

Bianca blew out her cheeks. "Of course I *am* upset, but..."

Melanie's lips parted. "You still think he's innocent? After all that's happened to this family since he's been dating Mom?"

"Over the years, Isaac's been in trouble. Then he stole from his own father," Bianca explained.

"What are you saying? He attacked Mom?" Melanie asked.

"I'm not sure. But if someone wanted to kill Mom, they would have done it. I wonder if the intruder was looking for something else."

Melanie swayed from side to side. "Looking for what, though?"

"That, I can't pinpoint," Bianca said.

"No!" her mother exclaimed.

Bianca and Melanie sprinted back to the breakfast table, to their mother, along with Lamar and Atkins. Deborah Wallace was running her fingers around her neck. Luther was looking at the floor. Why hadn't Bianca noticed before? Her mother's silver heart pendant was missing. Her gift from Luther was gone.

"It can't be gone," her mother whimpered.

"What happened?" Lamar asked.

"My necklace," her mother said, still feeling around her neck.

Luther rose to his feet and cupped her face in his hands. "We'll find it."

"Was something wrong with the clasp?" Melanie asked as she looked around the kitchen floor. Detective Atkins joined her, using his flashlight to check the tiled floor.

Her mother shook her head. "No. It never came off when I was wearing it. I had it on earlier, before I passed out."

Luther kissed the top of her head.

Her mother's voice quivered. "I'm so sorry. That was important to you."

"What matters is you're okay," Luther replied.

Bianca's lips parted. Was it possible that the intruder had taken her mother's necklace? Was that all they'd wanted, since they'd caused no physical harm? Why a necklace? What was so important about it? Bianca inhaled. She motioned to Lamar.

He raised an eyebrow but walked over to her.

"I'll get you some water," Luther said to Deborah.

"What's up?" Lamar asked Bianca.

She said, "You may shut me down, but in relation to Luther's case—"

"How?"

"He gave my mother that necklace. Why would someone steal a necklace? Why not take anything else? We didn't see a mess when we found her. They had one plan in mind and got what they wanted," she explained.

Lamar rubbed at his stubble-covered chin. "I won't say it's too farfetched, since nothing else was missing and they didn't seriously hurt your mother."

"Someone has it out for Luther," Bianca continued. "He's their target and... I wonder if he can lead us to them."

"'Us'?" Lamar tilted his head to the side.

"Okay, *you*, but you get what I mean," she said. "There's more behind this case. If Luther knows something, perhaps—"

"If he does, I'll ask him. Meanwhile, why not stay with your mother tonight?" Lamar suggested.

"Okay, but you'll consider what I said? Yes, my theories can be..."

"Interesting?"

She gave a faint smile. "That's a nice way of putting it."

He called out to Detective Atkins and the remaining officers with him. "Let's head out." He faced Bianca once more. "I'll have someone keep watch outside for your mother."

"Thank you." She could have kissed him, but held back. She didn't want an audience for their first kiss. "I appreciate you doing this."

Lamar, Detective Sims, and the EMTs left. Though they recommended a hospital checkup, her mother refused and signed a waiver. Melanie searched their mother's refrigerator for leftovers while Luther helped their mother to the sofa in her living room. Bianca met her sister in the kitchen.

"I'm staying tonight with Mom." Melanie looked over at Luther, who wrapped an arm around their mother's shoulders. "Not quite convinced yet that he's telling us everything."

Bianca said, "It's the perfect time to get the entire story." She didn't blame Melanie for being skeptical. Even she hadn't known what to think when she'd talked to Luther outside. If he'd kept this much from them now, was it possible he was hiding something else?

Melanie set the Tupperware on the kitchen island. Then she followed Bianca to the living room.

Luther cleared his throat at their arrival. "Have a seat, you two."

Melanie and Bianca sat on the opposite couch. What would he say? How much information would he give them about his past?

"I owe you an apology," he said, apparent regret in his furrowed brow. "Bringing harm to your family wasn't my intention. This wasn't supposed to happen."

Deborah Wallace gripped his hand. "None of this is your fault."

He shook his head. "My past, Deborah... I should've been more upfront with them." He faced Melanie and then Bianca. "I've been married twice before. I had one son with my first wife and a daughter with my second."

Melanie grazed her chin with her fingers as she listened.

Luther continued. "My first wife passed in an accident after we divorced. My second wife, Camille's mother, passed too." He blew out his cheeks. "Isaac's true identity has been a secret for a long time. When I was younger, I wasn't a real father to him or Camille. I wouldn't blame either of them if they never spoke to me again."

"Camille seemed ready to defend you with the police," Bianca said.

Luther gave her a faint smile. "She's been more open to reconcile than Isaac. He's all business, though we talk occasionally. He only took the manager's position at the car wash because he needed a job, especially with his past."

Deborah Wallace patted his hand. "You're making amends now. You don't have to blame yourself anymore."

He shook his head. "Someone broke into your house tonight, Deb." The affection in his voice had been apparent when he'd said his nickname for her. "I wish I knew who could have done this."

Bianca rubbed her lips together. He mentioned ex-wives. No help there. She couldn't talk to the deceased women.

Melanie cleared her throat. "I wish you were honest before, but thank you for telling us the truth."

"It'll take time," he said, "but I hope I can regain your trust."

Melanie didn't reply.

Bianca interjected. "I'm curious, Luther. You said your first wife died after her car went off the road?"

He bobbed his head. "That's what the police said. There was an empty bottle in her car, but they never recovered the body."

"How long ago was this?" Bianca asked.

He raised his eyebrows as he looked upward. "That was almost thirty years ago, Bianca."

"What are you getting at, Bianca?" her mother asked as her own forehead wrinkled.

"I'm not sure." She sat back on the couch. "Luther, do you have anything from your two previous marriages? Like mementos, letters, things like that?"

He shook his head. "Not that I can think of." Then he snapped his fingers. "There is a letter from Camille's mother. There was nothing in it, really, except a last goodbye after our divorce."

"Take me to your house. I'm wondering if we're overlooking something." She couldn't deny the hunch in her stomach.

"I'm going with you then," Melanie said, sprinting to her feet.

"No, stay here with Mom. Luther and I will handle this," she said.

"What do you expect to find?" her mother asked.

"Not sure," Bianca said.

Melanie took her arm and led her to the kitchen. "I'm not letting you go anywhere with him. What are you thinking, anyway?" she whispered.

"I don't know," Bianca whispered back. "I'm just trying to narrow down the possibilities. Someone broke into Mom's house. Her necklace is gone. Isaac is Luther's son. Camille admits to being at the car wash. There are too many options here. It's confusing." Even her theory of the creek being the crime scene didn't seem to carry much weight anymore. What if she was thrown off the killer's trail?

Melanie exhaled. "I still don't feel comfortable with you going with Luther."

"You don't trust him, but I believe he's telling the truth. My gut says this is all a setup. It's just a point of whom." She tilted her head to the side.

"You'll come back here when you're finished?" Melanie asked.

Bianca reassured her. "Yes. I'll text you if I find anything. If there's an emergency, call Lamar."

Chapter 25

Bianca had never been to Luther's ranch-style home before, but once she'd walked inside after him, the smell of coffee greeted her nose. Passing through the entryway, they entered the living room. An overstuffed chair with a throw blanket over the arm caught her eye. TV remotes cluttered the wooden coffee table, with the television mounted on the wall.

"What are you looking for?" He stacked his coasters on the coffee table.

"I'm not sure, but... is there a space where you keep important documents? There has to be a reason someone was after that necklace you gave Mom."

Luther rubbed the back of his head. "I have a home office with a small file cabinet. It's a backup for the books from the car wash."

Bianca followed him down the long hallway. She hadn't expected to encounter a wooden bookshelf filled with books and there was a corkboard on the wall with sheets of paper pinned. Bianca spotted her fundraiser flier on the board, along with one for the upcoming Summer Festival.

Screech! Luther had a time opening the first drawer of the file cabinet. "It's old."

Bianca gave a faint smile as she walked over next to him. Manila folders lined the drawer. "All of this is business?"

The thick papers rustled together as he thumbed through them. He nodded.

"Do you owe anyone money, Luther?"

"No, even during our slow months, we've never gone under."

Bianca pulled in her bottom lip. She opened her mouth to ask another question, but a white envelope caught her eye. "What's that?"

"What's what?" Luther replied.

"The letter?" Bianca pointed to it.

He grabbed it and opened it. Did he not remember? Why not share about this too? He sighed as he held it in his hands. "This is... this was from my first wife." His lips parted as if memories resurfaced. "I guess she put it in my bag before I left that day." He sniffled, but continued. "Oh man." He read aloud. "'*I'll never forgive you. I gave up everything to be with you and you deserted me.*'"

"'Gave up everything?' What did she mean?" Bianca asked.

"Her parents didn't approve, thinking I didn't deserve her." He released a less-than-humorous laugh. "I guess they were right."

"What was her name?"

He gave a faint smile. "Helen. Helen Moore... Gone too soon. She was so creative. I used to catch her drawing all the time. It didn't matter if it was a receipt or notebook paper. She would even hum the same old tune as she did it. I didn't care for the song at first, but it grew on me."

"What song was it? Do you remember?"

"1965. 'What the World Needs Now Is Love.' Whenever I came home, and she hummed that, I knew she was in her creative zone," Luther explained.

Bianca's heart squeezed, feeling compassion for him. Then she motioned to the door. "Let's keep looking, huh?"

Luther rolled his shoulders back and returned the letter to the drawer. They searched the rest of his home office, garage, and his kitchen but found nothing to share with the police. It was a dead end and Bianca had no answers to give.

Buzz. Buzz.

Taking her phone out of her pocket, she saw a message from Melanie.

Everything ok?

She didn't blame her for worrying.

Yes. We're fine. No clues yet.

She tucked her phone back in her pocket as she and Luther checked his entryway closet. Bianca had no idea what she was searching for. "Luther, do you mind if we check your bedroom?"

"Sure." He motioned for her to follow him. Once inside, she went to look under his full-sized bed. There were a few extra shoe boxes, but nothing worth paying attention to. Bianca blew out her cheeks. Perhaps this was a lost cause.

"Luther?" she called out as she straightened to rest her knees on his beige carpeted floor. "You don't have a safe, do you?"

"In my closet. I keep my most important files in there. Easier to grab in case of emergencies."

Sensible, like most people. "Would you notice if anything was missing? Could someone crack the code?"

"We can check, but no one knows it but me," he said.

"Let's make sure." Bianca rose to her feet and followed him to his closet. The woodsy scent of cologne filled her lungs. He had a few suits and pants on hangers and shoes lined one side of the carpeted floor. Bianca spotted the black safe in the right corner and she waited as Luther bent over to open it.

Click. He slid the door open, and she saw more manila folders inside, along with what looked like a purple drawstring bag.

"Anything missing?" she asked, wringing her hands together.

"Everything's here," he said.

Bianca stepped back, only to feel something underneath her shoe. Moving her foot and staring at the carpet, she blinked. She bent over to pick it up. It was the back of an earring.

"Luther," she said.

He closed the safe and straightened to his feet. "What's wrong?"

She held up the back of the rose gold earring to him. "What's this?" Did Luther have another woman?

His mouth dropped. "What *is* that?"

"It's part of a woman's earring... in your bedroom."

He raised his hands in surrender. "Before you get the wrong idea, I would never do that to your mother. I promise." He put his hands to his side and stared at the earring. "I don't recognize this at all."

Though it was easier to assume the worst of him, Bianca exhaled. Until the whole truth came out, she didn't want to jump to conclusions. Whoever was out to get Luther was definitely having everyone in Edenville question his character. "Okay." She'd let it go for now.

"But it proves one thing," he said.

"What?" she asked.

"Someone was in my house." He faced Bianca. "Who's responsible for all of this?"

"I don't know," Bianca replied, clutching the earring back in her hand. "I'm going to head back to my mother's house. I'll get an Uber to drive me."

He shook his head. "It's no problem, Bianca. I can take you—"

She held up her hand and stopped him. "It's okay, Luther. I'd rather take an Uber." She could use the time to reflect.

Luther didn't argue.

Bianca walked back to his living room after sending for her ride. She placed the back of the earring inside her pocket. Was it wise to tell Lamar? Should she wait until she had more evidence? Her shoulders dropped when she recalled her promise to him.

I found something at Luther's house. Sent.

She tapped her fingers on her phone. *Buzz. Buzz.* She figured he wouldn't waste time responding.

Why were you at Luther's house? He's only out on bail.

Call me crazy, but he's innocent. Bianca exited Luther's house and walked to the driveway. Lamar called her.

"Before you say anything," she said once she picked up, "I'm okay."

Silence.

"Lamar?" She tapped her flat shoe to the concrete. Thank goodness the street lights illuminated the surrounding area. Her Uber would arrive in five minutes.

"I heard you." He sighed. "What did you find?"

"I found the back of an earring."

"Your mother's?" he asked.

Bianca didn't consider that. It looked like it belonged to a stud. "No, my mother wears more dangling earrings. It's rare she wears studs."

"Another woman was in Luther's house?"

"He denies that he's seeing someone else," she replied.

"Bianca, the evidence against Luther can't be denied. He's out on bail. It's enough to stay away for a while."

That may have been true, but Bianca saw the remorse look on Luther's face. "He's tried so hard to make amends for his past. He knows the mistakes he's made. Why ruin all of it now? Kill a man only to get caught?"

"Some killers have another agenda. They want to look guilty so they can pull off a bigger plan," he explained.

"Like what?" she asked, not convinced at all.

Lamar exhaled. "Bianca, I've done my job, and that's the end of this case. Are you on your way home?"

She turned to see Luther staring at her through his window. She waved good night to him and slid into the back seat of the silver Toyota Camry Hybrid. "I'm on my way back to my mother's."

"Text me when you get there," Lamar said.

Bianca agreed. "Okay. I'll talk to you later." She hung up, not giving him the chance to say goodbye. His logical ways could get under her skin, so she breathed through her nose. Taking the earring back out of her pocket once more, she stared at it. "Excuse me?" She acknowledged the Uber driver.

"Yes?" he replied. He had a bald head with long fingers gripping the wheel.

"Can you take me to the police station instead? Can you cancel this ride and create a new one?" she asked. She didn't care if Lamar wanted her to go home. He wouldn't deny her hunch after hearing what she had to say.

Opening a new browser window on her phone, she typed in Susan Hayward's name. Would her jewelry business come up? Bingo! Bianca saw the link to *Hayward Jewels*. Then the store reviews caught her eye. Not quite what Bianca expected. *So cheap! Broke after one day of wearing!* Then another. *Why are these earrings so flimsy? Lost one already!*

Chapter 26

Bianca had pictured something quite different on Monday evening. The Uber driver dropped her off at the police station, and she dashed out to the front doors. Inside, phones still rang, keys jingled, and voices came over the intercom. Bianca approached the front desk, only to make eye contact with Lamar, who walked along with Detective Atkins.

He said a final word to Atkins. Lamar rubbed the back of his head when he approached Bianca. "You didn't go back to your mother's."

"I have something for you," she said.

"What?"

Her eyes shifted around. "Where's your desk? Can we sit?"

He bit the inside of his cheek but gestured her to follow him. Once they'd passed a few empty desks, they came to his. Lamar moved a few scattered files across the wooden desk and pointed to the seat across from him. Bianca obliged. "What's so important that it couldn't wait until tomorrow?" He rubbed at his eyes. "I'd planned on being home by now."

Bianca leaned over his desk. "It's about what I found at Luther's tonight."

"The earring, right? Are you sure it's not your mother's?" he repeated.

"I know it's not." She pulled it out of her pocket and showed it to him. "This was on the floor near Luther's safe."

He took it in his hand. "Is this related to Luther and this case?"

She swallowed. "I think I know whom it belongs to."

Lamar's brow furrowed. "I'm listening."

"I met a woman at the park. She's new in town. Her name is Susan Hayward. She lost the back of her earring and this reminds me of it."

He shrugged. "What's that got to do with Luther?"

"I'm not sure."

"All we can do is question her. The most she'll be guilty of is breaking and entering. Was anything else missing?"

"Not that Luther noticed. He found this letter from his first wife after he'd left her, but nothing else." Bianca's face slackened. "She..."

He laced his fingers together on top of his desk. "He told us about her accident. They never found the body, from what I researched."

Bianca sat back in her plastic chair. "Perhaps this was a long shot."

"What were you thinking?" Lamar asked.

She raised an eyebrow. "You *care* about my theories?"

"It's been a long day, so indulge me." He cracked a smile and his gray eyes flashed.

Bianca ignored the quiver in her stomach. "The case seems to be about getting Luther. Someone wants to tarnish his character. What if Susan knows someone who knew him? Perhaps his first ex-wife? What if it's all a part of a bigger scheme? Revenge?"

"What if this Susan Hayward knows something?" he asked.

"It's possible?" She pointed to the earring. "Is she working for someone to get Luther? That resembles her earring I saw the day of meeting her in the park. I helped her find it." Then Bianca snapped her fingers.

"What?" Lamar said.

"What if I talk to her? She's staying at the Stargaze Hotel. You wire me and if anything goes wrong, you can intervene," she suggested.

Lamar shook his head. "I'm not wiring you, Bianca, over what's possibly a simple break-in inside Luther's house. This Susan Hayward may not have any connection with this case."

"And what if she does?"

"I need more than one earring."

Bianca rested her elbows on his desk.

Lamar grabbed a pen and fiddled with it between his fingers.

Bianca grabbed her phone from her pocket. It was a long shot, but what if she found evidence online? People uploaded old news stories to YouTube every day. "The case with Luther's first wife was about thirty years ago, right?"

"Yes," Lamar replied through his clenched jaw.

Bianca typed in what she remembered. *1993. White woman goes off the cliff. Body never found.* While a few newspaper articles showed first on the search page, Bianca found a video. Clicking on it, she extended her hand for Lamar to watch with her.

A middle-aged white man reported the story. "This is Carver Andrews reporting for KG News giving you the latest in the tragic story that broke last night. Witnesses found twenty-eight-year-old Helen Burkes' car at the bottom of the famous Western Bluffs cliff, which is not that far from Lake Travis in Austin, Texas. They didn't discover the body, but police suspect she was thrown from the car and died at the scene. We'll have more breaking details as this story unfolds."

Bianca exited the video and searched for another. "I wonder if they have another segment with Luther. Did he do an interview?

"I didn't find one," Lamar said.

She figured he'd already looked.

"Bianca?" He placed a hand on hers to put her phone down. "I suggest you get some sleep and go to work tomorrow, as usual."

Her shoulders dropped. "I... thought I had something."

"I appreciate it, but there's nothing more we can do now. We've charged Luther. It's out of my hands," he said.

Bianca gazed at her phone once more to see if she spotted another video or article. She paused when she spotted another one about Helen's accident. This included a photo of her and Luther. It must have been during happier times in their marriage. Helen's skin looked smooth, and her smile was bright as one of her hands cupped Luther's face.

Bianca blinked and zoomed in on the photo. There was no way.

"Bianca?" Lamar waved a hand in front of her.

"Lamar..." She swallowed despite her dry mouth.

"What's wrong? You look like you've seen a ghost," he said.

That was an understatement. "We need to go to the Stargaze Hotel. Now."

"Bianca, I told you—"

She turned her phone to face him. "The police said they didn't find the body of Helen Burkes." She wasn't quite all the way sure herself. If she was right, this case had gotten even more interesting.

Chapter 27

Bianca ran her hands down the front of her shirt. There was no going back from here. She approached the front desk, greeted by the friendly receptionist with long strawberry blonde hair and violet eyes.

"Excuse me? Is Susan Hayward available?" she asked.

"I can call in and check. May I ask who's calling for her?" she wondered as she picked up the phone.

"I'm Bianca Wallace. A new friend. Tell her I'm the woman she met in the park the other day," Bianca said. Since she'd met Susan before, hopefully it wouldn't be a problem to ask hotel management for her room number.

The woman nodded. "Hello, Ms. Hayward, you have a visitor. Bianca Wallace. She said you met at the park. Yes. Okay, great." The woman hung up the phone. "You can go right up. She just ordered room service too, so she said you can join her. Room 429."

"Thank you," Bianca said, as she walked to the elevators. *Ping.* She entered once the metallic doors had opened. Thank God she was the only one inside the elevator. Most of the guests had turned in already, she assumed.

"Can you hear me?" Lamar said into her earpiece.

Bianca adjusted it inside her ear. "Yes. Things good on your end?"

"Yes. Detective Atkins will be in the hallway if something goes wrong. Got that?" Lamar said.

"Got it," she said. How would she do this? What if she was wrong? Was it only a coincidence?

"Are you okay?" he asked.

She smiled at his thoughtfulness. "I'm okay, Lamar. I'll be fine."

"Okay. Let's hope you're right about this."

Me too. *Ping.* The automated doors opened, and Bianca entered the long hallway. There was a sign in front of her that showed room numbers. Room 429 was to her left. She swallowed with each step she took.

Squaring her shoulders, Bianca faced Room 429. *Knock. Knock.* She shifted her head to either side, only to spot Detective Atkins at the end of the hallway. He stood next to the door that led to the stairs. He gave her a thumbs-up and Bianca bobbed her head in response.

Susan answered the door with a smile. "Bianca? Welcome. I'm surprised you're here."

Bianca ignored the tightness in her chest. Susan's welcoming personality had her second-guessing herself, but what if this stranger could tell her something? "I hope it's not a bad time." She checked the watch on her wrist. "It's getting late." Time showed it was almost nine o'clock at night.

Susan waved her hand away and invited her inside. "Nonsense. I'm having a late dinner, anyway. Join me."

Bianca walked past the bathroom to her left and entered Susan's room. The hotel's queen-sized bed was to the right. The air conditioner hummed, and she bypassed the closet with non-removable hangers.

"Have a seat." Susan pointed to the small chair while she sat in the office chair at the wooden desk. "What brings you here? To convince me to stay for the summer festival in town?" She cocked her head to the side. "I'm considering it."

Bianca smiled. "You'd enjoy it." Now for her reason for showing up. "I know you're retired, but could you replicate jewelry pieces?" She pointed to her wrist, going along with her made-up story. "My daughter got me this bracelet. Can you replicate it so we'll match? I could buy one from the store, but I'd like the personal touch." Bianca held up her arm, showing Susan her charm bracelet.

Susan's eyes brightened. "This is beautiful." She grabbed a piece of paper from the stationery on the desk. "What type of charms would you want on hers?"

A *tsk* escaped Bianca's lips. "Her phone. It's practically attached to her hand."

Susan giggled as she drew with her pencil. "I can understand that. What else? Things that reflect her personality?"

"Music. Dogs. Art. Dessert," Bianca said. "Are you sure this isn't putting you out? I only wanted to ask."

"Nonsense, dear," Susan replied. "I love special projects." She winked at her. "Keeps the skill fresh in my mind."

"You got into this after your first marriage?" Bianca pointed to her bare ring finger. "I'm divorced too."

Susan paused her drawing. Her face softened. "I'm sorry." She released a deep sigh. "Yes, during and after it ended. That... broke my heart. I never remarried. But... life goes on." She tucked a loose hair behind her ear with her scarred hand.

Bianca was about to ask another question, but she overheard Susan humming. It was faint at first, but the melody became clear. "What the World Needs Now Is Love." Luther's words replayed in her mind. *"Whenever I came home, and she hummed that, I knew she was in her creative zone."*

Bianca had studied the photos of young Helen Burkes at the police station with Lamar. Who else was aware she was alive? She'd kept it a secret along with creating another identity. Thirty years and leaving her son behind.

Bianca leaned in to see Susan's drawing, not quite ready to give herself away. Hairs raised on the back of her neck, though, because of the revelation.

Susan picked up the stationery with her mock drawing. "Well?"

Bianca's lips parted at the drawing that resembled her own bracelet. Susan was talented. "Amazing."

Susan touched her scarred hand to her chest.

"What's wrong?" Bianca asked.

Susan's hand traveled from her chest to her throat. "Nothing, only a... memory I'd like to forget." She motioned to the drawing. "How about this?"

A knot twisted in Bianca's stomach. "It's beautiful, but..." Sweat built on her palms, but she pushed through the nerves. A man's freedom depended on it. "One more question. How did you... survive the car crash, thirty years ago... Helen?"

Susan's eyes bugged. "What?" She shot to her feet, allowing the drawing to fall to the carpeted floor. "What did you call me?"

Bianca swallowed. "You're Helen Burkes. Luther Burkes's first wife. Aren't you?" She unlocked her phone and showed her the photo she'd seen at the police station. Susan—Helen—had Luther's youthful face cupped next to hers, using her scarred hand.

Susan shook her head vigorously. "What makes you presume I'm this *Helen* woman?"

Bianca pointed to her scarred hand. "It's in the same place. Plus, you hummed that song as you were drawing."

"I hum every time I draw. It gets me—"

"In the *creative zone*." Bianca finished her sentence. "Luther said that's what you did."

Susan shuffled backward. "How dare you come here and *accuse* me of being someone else. Who is this woman?"

"It's okay, Helen. You only have to tell the truth."

Susan waved her statement away, clearly struggling to find the right words. "What are you talking about? I invited you here as a friendly gesture, but it's obvious you have me confused with this *Helen* woman. She died a long time ago when her car went off the cliff! Now, will you please get out?" She pointed to the door.

Bianca slipped her phone back into her pocket. "Susan... I didn't tell you about Helen's car. How did you know that?"

"I can't read news stories?" she argued.

"From 1993? That specific story?"

Susan's facial features slackened. She gripped her scarred hand. "No, you didn't say that." She looked upward at the ceiling. "I... forgot about that picture of us."

"Bianca," Lamar said in her earpiece. "Keep her talking."

Bianca asked Helen, "What happened? You faked your own death?"

Susan—Helen—paced the floor. "It wasn't a secret that I drank. Why not use it to my advantage? Luther, he..." Her posture stiffened saying his name. "You said they respect him in this town." She shook her head. "He was *selfish*."

"And Isaac? Your son?"

"He still thinks I'm dead, but when the private investigator said he was here... working for Luther. I had to come. I hadn't had the chance to tell him." Helen's jaw clenched. "But I needed his father out of the way."

"How did you escape the accident unscathed?" Bianca asked.

"Hardly anyone visited Western Bluffs at night. I'd left Isaac with a babysitter. Luther had left, saying he wanted a divorce. It broke me. I didn't know what I was doing, but I hit the gas. When my car soared off the cliff, I jumped into the water. As the fastest swimmer on my team in high school, I could get away fast. I left my identification in the car along with the liquor bottle. I bought a bus ticket with cash and left," Helen said.

"But you left your son behind." Bianca mentioned.

Helen raked her fingers through her hair. "I'd planned on getting him back, but the timing had to be right. My parents were aware of what I did, so they sought custody of Isaac. The plan was to give Isaac to me unofficially. Then they told me Luther got him. That's when... I foiled my plan."

"You wanted to kill Luther?" Bianca wondered. "All these years?" Talk about bitterness.

Helen shook her head. "I thought about it. Killing him was too easy. When I found about his daughter's ex-husband... The problems they were having..." She gave a mirthless laugh. "It was perfect. The time had come. Send Luther to prison and let the justice system deal with him. Especially if *all* the evidence points to him."

Bianca's lips parted. "You... killed Ronald?" How was that possible without Luther knowing?

"Hiring a private investigator got me all the information I needed. I kept a close eye on Luther. I saw the fight with Ronald and Camille. Luther came out with a gun. He had Camille leave, so she didn't see me. Luther and Ronald fought, a few shots fired, but no one appeared hurt. Then I saw Luther get knocked out.

I called Bruce and told him to get Ronald to meet him at the creek again. Ronald left to meet his brother, and I picked up Luther's gun since he was still unconscious. I met Bruce at the creek because it was better than being out in the open. It was time to enact our plan. I arrived just in time to see the brothers arguing about Camille. I shot Ronald, and we took his body back to the wash bay. Then I put the gun back in Luther's hand. He still hadn't come to," she explained.

"How did you get away from the crime scene?" Bianca wondered.

Helen tilted her head. "Bruce of course." Her shoulders drooped. "If he wasn't so stuck on Camille, he probably wouldn't have gotten involved. He wanted to get rid of his brother for good. Camille had always confided in him about Ronald, so Bruce finally had enough."

"So you two... plotted this together," Bianca said. "What about my mother's necklace?" She couldn't forget that. Was it her or Bruce who pulled that job?

"That was Bruce too. He also got into your office." Helen sneered, boring her eyes into Bianca's. "I couldn't believe Luther got *her* a necklace, too. Anyway, I threw it away in a dumpster."

Bianca's lips pulled back in disgust. "How dare you? My mother had nothing to do with—"

"That's *enough* of the questions. Don't you think?" Helen blew out her cheeks. "Well... this was not in my plan. But I can improvise."

"I'm coming, Bianca," Lamar said in her ear.

Thud. Thud. Thud. Thud. It had to be Detective Atkins.

In a flash, Helen grabbed a gun from the nearby drawer. Pointing it at Bianca. She raised her hands in a gesture of surrender.

Chapter 28

"You don't want to do this." Bianca sat on the queen-sized bed.

Helen shook her head. "I've waited thirty years for this, Bianca. I'm not giving up now."

"Open the door!" Detective Atkins shouted. "Police! Open up!"

"Bianca?" Lamar said in her earpiece.

Despite her gut tightening, Bianca continued. "Helen, think of what you're doing. I know Luther hurt you, but you've wasted your life creating this cruel fantasy of revenge. I'm sorry your marriage didn't work out. But you can't—"

"Shut up! Just shut up!" Helen roared.

"If you don't open the door, we're going to break it down!" Detective Atkins yelled.

Helen shouted back. "Do that and I'll shoot her!"

Bianca flinched, keeping her hands in the air. Then a familiar voice permeated the door.

"Helen Burkes," Lamar said, "this is Detective Sims. No one else has to get hurt. Okay? Tell us what you want."

Helen smirked. "Luther Burkes. Tell him to get here *now*! Or his future step-daughter dies."

Bianca's blood chilled, but she rested her hands on either side of the bed.

"Okay, Helen," Lamar replied. "We'll get Luther here. We're calling him now."

Helen smiled. "Finally, men who get things done."

Bianca tried again. "Helen... why do you want Luther here?"

"Closure. I sacrificed everything for him. I could have made more money if I'd started my business earlier. But no. I married him. I almost lost my relationship with my parents because of him. Then he leaves? Suddenly, I'm not what he wants anymore?" She sniffled, but no tears came. "No. He *deserves* what's coming to him."

"I get it," Bianca said. "It happened when my husband left. He even remarried."

Helen's jaw clenched.

"The pain is real. I cried myself to sleep for a long time, but I healed. I didn't want to live that way anymore. There was my daughter to think about. Helen, what about your son? If he hasn't seen you since he was a boy, wouldn't you like to tell him you're alive?" Bianca added.

"I've seen him." Helen's voice sounded shaky, but she spoke, anyway. "I have photos of him from the private investigator."

"That's not the same. What about hugging and telling him you love him. How much you've missed him all these years," she replied. Bianca assumed by Helen's watering eyes her words were affecting her. Then a sneer followed.

Helen's eyes looked wild-eyed. "Don't you understand? I've come *too far*. Once Luther gets here, that'll be the end of it."

What else could Bianca say? Helen was a desperate woman who'd planned revenge against her ex-husband. She'd even put Bianca's mother in harm's way.

"What about your family?" Bianca asked. "Do they know you're alive?"

Helen's eyes narrowed at her. "They did. They're dead now."

Bianca decided not to poke the bear any further. Obviously, Helen had nothing to lose.

"Bianca, don't worry," Lamar said in her earpiece. "We'll get you out. I promise."

"Helen?" Lamar called out from the hallway. "He's here."

Helen walked to the door, and Bianca didn't take her eyes off her. How much time had passed, anyway? The minutes appeared to tick slowly with a gun in the room. Bianca had sat in silence for a while. How much longer would Helen wait to shoot her? For her to go this far, it wouldn't surprise Bianca if she killed Luther, too.

"Luther?" Helen called out.

"Helen? Is-It-How-Is it really you?" he stammered in apparent disbelief.

"Yeah. It's me. Only you can come in." She opened the door, pointing him ahead of her, and Luther slipped inside.

His eyes widened. "Bianca?"

Helen gestured for him to sit next to her.

"Helen, what are you doing?" he asked, his forehead furrowed.

"Hello to you too, *dear*," she said, wetting her lips. "You've grown a beard."

Bianca tapped her fingers on her pant leg.

Luther held up his hands, as if to calm her down. "Helen, don't do anything rash. Okay? The police say if you surrender peacefully—"

"Why should I?" She pointed the gun at his face. "There's only one thing I want. An apology from you."

Luther opened his mouth. "Helen—"

"Apologize, Luther!" she yelled at him.

Bianca wanted to hide from the sense of impending doom.

"Okay. I'm sorry... I ruined your life. I can't change the past, but can you find it in your heart to... forgive me? Please?" he asked, despite the tremor in his voice.

Bianca shifted her eyes between the both of them. Helen didn't move, though she held the gun steady.

"Did you ever love me? Was any of it real to you?" she asked him, as her eyes shimmered with fresh tears.

"I did, Helen," Luther answered. "I loved you and it broke me when I heard about your accident."

Helen's face brightened. "Then let's get out of here. You, me, and Isaac."

Bianca held back her response.

"Helen..." Luther said. "I can't. I have a life here."

Helen pointed the gun back at Bianca. "We'll get rid of her and get by the police. Get Isaac. You, me, and our son. The way it was *supposed* to be."

"Bianca," Lamar said in her earpiece. "We're looking for another way inside. Atkins is still at the door. I'm coming through the balcony window."

Bianca didn't dare look outside. She kept her attention on Helen and the gun.

Luther stood up with his hands still in the air. "Helen, we can't do this. Turn yourself in. It's the right thing to do."

Her eyes burned with anger. "It's because of her. That woman you're with now! You love her, don't you?"

Luther attempted to reason with her. "Helen—"

"Don't you start!" she screamed at him.

Bianca's eyes shifted to the window. Lamar had a chair in his hand. How fast could Bianca roll onto the floor out of the clear shot of Helen's gun?

"Yes," Luther admitted. "I love her."

"Then I have nothing else to say to you." She pointed the gun back at his face now. "I think she'll be better off without you. You'll be glad I didn't kill her, but she'll *never* see you again."

Bianca grabbed a pillow and threw it at Helen's face, knocking her off-balance. Luther grabbed for the gun. *Crash!* Bianca rolled off the bed to the floor as glass shattered from the balcony window.

"I hate you!" Helen screamed as she and Luther wrestled.

POW! POW! Bianca covered her ears, but she heard the door break down. It had to be Detective Atkins, along with the other officers present.

Bianca shut her eyes despite the commotion. She only prayed Luther wouldn't get hurt.

"Bianca? Bianca!" Lamar called out.

She didn't move.

"I hate you!" Helen screamed, but her cries grew fainter.

Bianca opened her eyes and lifted her gaze to see Detective Atkins dragging her out of the room. Her eyes shifted to Luther, who bent over his knees. He handed Helen's gun to another officer.

"Bianca?" Lamar fell to his knees, cupping her hands with his. "Bianca, talk to me. Are you okay?" He took the earpiece out of her ear and stuffed it into his pocket.

Bianca's hands shook. It all happened so fast, she needed to gather her thoughts. "What?"

Lamar eyeballed her. "Are you okay?"

She touched his stubble-covered face. "I'm okay."

His eyes softened. "For a second there, I thought..."

"I promise. I'm all right."
He hugged her tightly, pressing a kiss to her neck.
Bianca didn't want to be this far away from him again.

Chapter 29

Bianca resumed her seat on the queen-sized bed in Helen's hotel room. With a thin blanket wrapped around her shoulders, she breathed easier. Luther gave his statement to Detective Atkins while a few officers inspected the room, taking pictures. Another close call with a killer and Bianca knew she wouldn't forget it.

"How are you holding up?" Lamar asked, sitting next to her.

She wrapped the blanket tighter around herself. "I'm still in shock. Helen... faked her own death." She turned to face Lamar. "And then Bruce..."

Lamar said, "He's the man she sold her jewelry business to, and she offered to pay him more once she discovered the connection he had to Luther's daughter, Camille. Thanks to her private investigator's thoroughness. Bruce's additional motivation? Camille, freeing her once and for all from Ronald. He propositioned Susan with, 'Kill my brother for me and we'll frame your ex for it. We'll both benefit.'"

A feather could have knocked Bianca over. "Wow."

"Camille even told us at the police station Ronald suspected they were having an affair," he explained.

"Did they?" Bianca wondered.

"Camille denied it," Lamar answered.

Bianca scratched the back of her head. "What about the wristwatch I found?"

"Bruce admitted to meeting up with his brother at the creek the day before. Ronald lost the watch then in their scuffle. The night of the killing, Bruce called and lied to Ronald, saying he had information about Camille. The brothers exchanged words and Helen shot him at the creek and they brought his body back to a still unconscious Luther," he continued.

A flush of adrenaline tingled through Bianca's body. "When I saw that photo... I saw the scar on her hand. Then when she hummed the song like Luther said Helen used to do, that proved it."

Lamar nudged her shoulder. "Good work."

Did she hear that correctly? "What? You're telling me 'good job,' detective?"

He chuckled. "Don't let it go to your head, okay? But, you came through—again. Ever wondered about consulting for the police department? You may have missed your calling."

Bianca replied, "No, I'll stick with graphic design. Helping now and then is one thing, but doing it full time? Nah."

"Give it some thought," Lamar said. "I'm sure the chief at headquarters won't mind. It impressed him how you figured out Sherry Wilson's murder case."

Bianca's chest expanded with pride as she removed the blanket from her shoulders. "Thank you. I'll keep it in mind."

He leaned in closer. "I usually discourage you, but if you're going to get involved, at least the department can back you up. We can only do so much with a nosy civilian."

Bianca's mouth dropped. "*Nosy*? I've been helpful."

Buzz. Buzz. She grabbed her phone from her pocket. Her mother and sister were outside. Telling them the news over the phone hadn't been easy, but her mother and Melanie were glad she didn't get hurt.

Lamar motioned to the door. "You can leave if you need to."

"Okay." She stood.

Lamar did the same. "I'll walk you downstairs," he said, motioning to Detective Atkins.

Bianca held up a hand, walking over to Luther, who stood in the corner.

He gave a faint smile. "Are you all right?"

She smiled. "I am. You?"

Luther's gaze appeared unfocused. Bianca didn't blame him for being in disbelief. "I will be, but... I never figured Helen would... do something like this."

Bianca touched his arm. "Are you going to tell Isaac?"

He bobbed his head. "I hate for him to know his mother did this, but I'm not holding back the truth anymore."

Bianca embraced him, and he returned the gesture. "I'm glad you're all right."

He patted her back. "I'm glad you are too."

She pulled back. "I'll see you at the fundraiser? Not going to let this ruin the cause, are you?"

"Of course not." He winked at her, and Bianca backed away, joining Detective Sims at the door.

A few spectators stood in the hallway. After all the commotion and gunshots, they had drawn a crowd. Bianca walked to the nearest elevator, followed by Lamar. *Ping.* They entered inside alone. Faint elevator music played and Bianca stared at the operation panel once she'd pushed the button for the lobby.

Lamar cleared his throat. "Are you sure you're okay?"

"Yes." She wrung her hands together, only to feel his strong fingers on top of hers. There was no way he would kiss her now, but her quivering gut almost hoped he would. Linking her fingers through his, he held her hand for the rest of the elevator ride, and when the door opened, he released his firm grip.

They exited the elevator and entered the hallway. Bianca focused on the loud voice coming from the front desk.

The receptionist attempted to calm someone down. "I understand, but you can't go up. But I can tell the police you're here."

"This is ridiculous." She exhaled. "My daughter is up there. I—"

"Bianca!" Melanie yelled, running to her side.

Deborah Wallace touched a hand to her chest. Then she faced the receptionist. "Forgive me, won't you?"

Bianca clung to her sister.

"Are you all right?" Melanie stepped back to look at her.

Her mother moved in for a hug next. "I thought I was in a Lifetime movie."

"I'm okay. We got the actual killer." Bianca faced her mother. "Luther's innocent."

"So what happened?" Melanie asked. "Who did it?"

"His first wife *faked* her death," Lamar said. "She's been planning her revenge on him for years."

Deborah Wallace gasped. "Where is he? Can I see him?"

"He's answering a few questions for us," Lamar chimed in.

"Wow," Melanie said, touching a hand to her forehead.

"Wow" was right. The elevators pinged once more and this time, Detective Atkins entered the hallway, followed by Luther. Bianca's mother rushed into his arms and held him close.

"Excuse me, ladies," Lamar said when he spotted the hotel manager.

"I guess I was wrong," Melanie said.

Bianca nudged her sister's shoulder. "You wanted to protect Mom. We both did."

"Yeah, but... I assumed the worst." She looked over at the older couple holding each other close. "I'm glad the truth came to light, though."

"Me too," Bianca said, rubbing at her shoulders. She focused her eyes on Lamar. He'd rescued her once again. Before, she would have presumed he cared because of his job. The way he'd held her after Helen's gun had gone off, she hadn't felt that safe in a long time.

Despite her clammy hands, she couldn't keep her feelings to herself anymore. Though not ideal to share her heart at a crime scene, she would tell him. Sooner rather than later.

Epilogue

That weekend, Saturday afternoon, Luther's car wash brought in support from all of Edenville. With the murder charges against him dropped, people lined up to donate to his noble cause of supporting the local veterans. Susan—Helen—had been arrested. Bianca still couldn't fathom the woman had been living under an alias for thirty years. Planning and plotting her revenge against Luther for breaking her heart all those years ago. Even giving up her son to do it.

Using Bruce as an accomplice, because of his love for Camille, Susan had coerced him into taking Camille's car to run Bianca over, though he'd missed, and breaking into her office. Scare tactics to get her unraveled, since Helen had heard the rumors of Bianca's own investigation. On their way to the hospital, Bruce had almost hit them, too. Reckless driving on his part.

Yet, they hadn't counted on Bianca learning Helen's secret. The necklace reminded her of the one Luther gave her during their marriage, but she lost it after her attempted accident. Seeing a lookalike on another woman triggered her all the more.

It had shocked Isaac to learn his mother was still alive, and when he'd learned the truth, he hadn't wanted the strain between him and his father anymore. They'd had a professional relationship since he'd needed a job because of his past record with the law. Their personal relationship was another story. Bianca's heart warmed, knowing they were making amends. Camille's daughter, Lucy, had arrived in town earlier that afternoon. Luther's eyes lit up to see another image of his daughter, and Lucy didn't mind embracing her grandfather.

Bianca sipped her chilled cup of water as she listened to "Sh-Boom" by The Chords in the background. She didn't mind the classics playing, and by the looks of her mother dancing with Luther, they were having a ball. He'd given her a new necklace, too.

A mix of employees and townsfolk conversed as cars went through the automated wash. Melanie, Jordan, Judy, and even Richard were a few of the volunteers passing out water and serving mini burgers with fries. The cool breeze eased the heat, and since it was just the start of summer, Bianca took for granted the somewhat pleasant weather. Between the car wash and the summer festival today, Edenville had a busy weekend. Casper and her mother's dogs were with the dog sitter.

"Taking a break?" a familiar voice asked.

She met Lamar's gray eyes. "Needed some water, but I'm all right."

His choice of clothing today wasn't the usual suit and tie for work. Instead, he wore khaki shorts with a fitted cotton shirt and tennis shoes. Bianca liked his casual looks.

"Good turnout?" he said.

She nudged his shoulder. "Thanks to my amazing fliers."

Lamar laughed. "I agree you did a good job. When's your grand reopening?"

"Thank you. It'll be in two weeks. I have Veronica planning it, but my mother and sister want to help."

"They believe in you and want to see you succeed," he said.

"Thank you." She gulped the last of her water and tossed it in a nearby trashcan.

Lamar took her free hand. "You got a minute?"

She shifted her eyes for a moment. Did anyone need her? No one caught her eye, so she fell in step with Lamar and walked with him to the back of the building. Secluded.

She asked, "Something wrong?"

Releasing her hand, Lamar raised his eyebrow. "No. Nothing's wrong. I... I've been thinking a lot about... us."

Bianca's smile grew.

"I know I've been busy—" he started.

"I understand," she said to reassure him. "We're learning how to do..." She gestured between them. "This."

That caught his attention. "You want to, Bianca?"

Her heart pounded, but it was now or never. "I... haven't been in a relationship since my divorce. It's not like men didn't show interest, but I wasn't ready."

He took her hand in his again.

She continued. "It wasn't all my fault. Sometimes these things happen, even if we go into it with the best intentions." Bianca's bottom lip trembled. "I felt like a failure, but I knew I had to keep going for my daughter. Then... I met you and..." She shrugged. "I haven't had strong feelings for someone in years."

The corners of his mouth quirked up. "Me, neither. I wasn't counting on you, Bianca, but if you're willing, I'd like to see where this goes. I don't want to pursue anyone else. Only you. I can't promise perfection, but you'll *never* question how I feel about you."

She released his hands, only to bring them to his stubble face.

His breath caught at her touch. "Are you sure?"

She inched in closer. "Yes." Her voice was audible, but she mentally forced the tightness in her chest to loosen. One word flooded her mind. Bravery. To move forward in a new way. She'd already made progress on her own. She'd done the work to heal and forgive herself. Now was her time. Regardless of how things worked out, she wasn't running away. Not from life. Not from Lamar.

He embraced her waist, caressing her back. "I don't care if my phone rings or what. I'm *kissing* you this time."

"Please do." She tilted her head and his lips touched hers. Bianca held back her gasp. He didn't rush her, but pecked her mouth gently.

Wrapping her arms around his neck, she stood on her tiptoes to get closer. Lamar's hand rubbed her back as his kiss deepened. Bianca almost fainted with the static filling her brain, but she allowed him to hold her up. Her insides shivered as her heart burst with emotions.

Lamar moaned against her lips. He kissed one corner of her mouth and trailed more kisses back to the center of her lips. Her hands pulled him in closer, desiring to erase all distance between them.

Bianca smiled against his lips, liking the influence she had over him.

"I've been waiting for this for a long time," he whispered.

"Me too." She exhaled. "Thanks for being patient with me."

"You're worth it, Bianca. Ugh. Do we have to go back?" he asked, pressing his forehead to hers.

She touched her hand to his wrist as one of his hands caressed her cheek. "I think we do. But... we'll have more moments like this."

"I can't wait." He kissed her lips one more time. "One more minute?"

Bianca obliged and kissed him back, leaning into his touch. The world could wait for now...

To be continued in *Most Eligible Killer*

More by Crimson Fox Publishing

Enchantments and Escape Rooms (Spooky Games Club Mysteries, Book 2) by Amy McNulty

After the disaster of the month before, Dahlia Poplar, cursed witch and helper extraordinaire, is ready for her serene, supernatural small town life to return to normal. However, her hopes for a more peaceful existence don't last when a childhood friend moves back to Luna Lane to open up an escape room.

With the Spooky Games Club thriving, Dahlia decides to help her friend by using her magic to quickly get his business up and running. Dahlia's enchantments accomplish the task, but before the Games Club has a chance to enjoy the new attraction, a test of the escape room results in a freak, fatal accident. Riddled with guilt, Dahlia wonders where her enchantments went wrong—or if there's something more to the disaster.

The only way to divine whether or not the death was her fault, the result of an accident, or murder is to investigate—and perhaps even play the dangerous game herself. In this one-hour escape room, failure to escape could mean death, not just for Dahlia, but for those she holds most dear.

Read it now!

OLD FLAMES **(Northwest Magic, Book 2) by Elisa Keyston**

Laney isn't looking for love. She's perfectly happy with the life she's built for herself in the little town of Foreston, Washington. She's a successful businesswoman, the owner of an alterations shop with a clientele across the northwest. She's the chair of the local Victorian house museum's annual fashion show. And she has a reputation for a magic touch: the rumor around town is that anyone who wears one of the period costumes she designs in her spare time will be blessed with good luck.

That's what they say, anyway. Laney knows the truth is a bit more complicated—anything she wills while sewing has a tendency of coming to pass. It's a supernatural gift from the fae who are said to inhabit the woods surrounding the Paine Estate, and it's taught her to keep a guard on her notorious redheaded temper. But keeping her temper becomes difficult when journalist Paul Nelson comes to town to do a feature about the museum. With his stunning good looks and swoon-worthy English accent, Paul is charming, irresistible... and just so happens to be Laney's ex.

Laney wants nothing more than to keep Paul at arm's length, but when she stumbles across a series of break-ins at the museum, she may have no choice but to trust the dashing reporter who once broke her heart to help her catch the culprit. And when a nearby forest fire threatens the safety of the town—and of the woods—will Laney be able to put her old feelings aside in order to protect the magic of Foreston? Or will that same magic lead to an unexpected happy ending?

Read it now!

About the Author

Daria started writing as a teenager. Since she loves sweet romance novels, she figured why not write them too? Then she shifted in 2020 and now includes cozy mysteries and Christian fiction in her primary genres. Daria writes what comes to mind, so don't be surprised when you read something different. She graduated with a degree in healthcare management, so writing was not in the cards for her. It's rare that you won't catch her reading. Aside from that, she loves Turner Classic Movies, painting, Pilates, the piano, and chocolate.

More Books by Daria

Christmas Therapy https://books2read.com/u/b5Q1rA
The Wedding Report https://books2read.com/u/31Gow6
Christmas Connection https://books2read.com/u/bMpYRV
Wish for Love https://books2read.com/u/49oyNd

Stay in Touch

My website: www.dariawhite.com[1] Subscribe to my newsletter! Here you'll also get invited to my exclusive Facebook Group, **Daria's VIP Reader Circle**[2]. Want to interact with me more? Get on my mailing list for a VIP invite! I'd love to have you!

Follow me on Twitter: www.twitter.com/Daria_White15[3]

Follow me on Instagram: www.instagram.com/dariawhite90[4]

Bookbub: https://www.bookbub.com/profile/daria-white

---

1. http://www.dariawhite.com

2. **https://www.facebook.com/groups/dariavips/**

3. http://www.twitter.com/Daria_White15

4. http://www.instagram.com/dariawhite90

Thank You from Daria

Thank you again for reading *Lather. Rinse. Murder*! With recent life changes, this release took longer but I'm glad I didn't rush the process. I thank God for His grace, allowing me to keep going.

If you enjoyed this story, please take a few minutes to leave a rating or a review at your favorite retailer. If it's only a few words, it's perfectly fine with me. Unbelievably, it helps other readers to decide if they want to read my work or not. I look forward to sharing the next story with you. There's more to come!

God Bless,

Daria

Shout Outs!

WWW.VILADESIGN.NET[1] (Tatiana, you're the best and deliver every time!). To my family, your support and belief in me means so much. To my writing partners, you rock! I love bouncing ideas with you and you're always willing to give me amazing feedback. To my

---

1. http://www.viladesign.net

ARC team, I appreciate you taking the time to read *Lather. Rinse. Murder* in advanced. Your early reviews make such a difference!

To all of my fans, your support is a blessing. It's my pleasure to bring a new story to you. Thank you for reading whatever I choose to write!

Don't miss out!

Visit the website below and you can sign up to receive emails whenever Daria White publishes a new book. There's no charge and no obligation.

https://books2read.com/r/B-A-YNYJ-XBRFC

BOOKS2READ

Connecting independent readers to independent writers.

Did you love *Lather. Rinse. Murder*? Then you should read *The Wedding Report* by Daria White!

A writing career is Chantelle Woods' dream. To prove she's not just a pretty face, she agrees to profile the wedding of the year for her magazine: The Taylor Wedding. By traveling back to her hometown, Chantelle has one problem. Her ex is the groom. It's been ten years since she's talked to Lance, and following him around for a month doesn't sound promising. Working with him has her thinking about the mistake she made when she left, and what would have happened if she'd stayed.Lance Taylor is working to be a partner in his father's law firm. Despite being career-oriented, he shocked the world when he announced his engagement after years of bachelorhood. When he learns that his first love is profiling him for the story, he knows it will only stir up trouble. He can't afford the risk.There's no denying the magnetism between Lance and Chantelle, but the past is too painful to rehash. As his wedding day approaches, they both have to decide their fate. Go their separate ways for good or see if there's a second chance for love.